THE WINTER GUEST

Born in Glasgow, Sharman Macdonald becaɪ
graduation from Edinburgh University but gave ɪc up in order to
write. Her plays include: *When I Was a Girl . . .* which won her the
Evening Standard Award for Most Promising Playwright of 1984
and ran in London for one year; *The Brave*, 1988; *When We Were
Women*, 1988 (National Theatre); *All Things Nice*, 1991 (The Royal
Court); *Shades*, 1992 (Albery Theatre); *The Winter Guest*, 1994
(West Yorkshire Playhouse, The Almeida); *Borders of Paradise*,
1995 (Watford Palace); and *Sea Urchins*, 1996 (Catherine Bailey
Ltd for Radio Three). Her novels, *The Beast* and *Night, Night,*
have been published by Collins. She has written a film script, *Wild
Flowers*, which was filmed for Channel Four.

Alan Rickman has worked extensively in contemporary theatre,
including appearances at the Royal Court Theatre, Bush Theatre
and Hampstead Theatre. His portrayal of Valmont in *Les Liaisons
Dangereuses* took him from the West End to Broadway where he
was nominated for a Tony Award. He went on to make his film
début in *Die Hard*. Subsequent film appearances have included
Prince of Thieves for which he won a BAFTA Award, Stephen
Poliakoff's *Close My Eyes* and Anthony Minghella's *Truly Madly
Deeply*. For these films he was named Evening Standard Film
Actor of the Year. Other film credits include *Bob Roberts*, and,
most recently, *Sense and Sensibility* and *Michael Collins*, for both of
which he received BAFTA nominations. For his performance in
HBO's *Rasputin*, Rickman won Golden Globe, Emmy and SAG
awards.
   Alan Rickman directed the play of *The Winter Guest* at the
Almeida Theatre, London, and at the West Yorkshire Playhouse;
this is his feature film directorial début.

THE WINTER GUEST
Sharman Macdonald
and
Alan Rickman

ff6

faber and faber

First published in 1998
by Faber and Faber Limited
3 Queen Square London WC1N 3AU

Photoset by Parker Typesetting Service, Leicester
Printed in England by Clays Ltd, St Ives plc

A CIP record for this book
is available from the British Library
ISBN 0-571-19479-6

NOTE
This edition represents the original shooting
script rather than that of the completed film.

2 4 6 8 10 9 7 5 3 1

CREDITS

EXT. THE FIELD. MORNING

Frozen earth. A field. Ploughed ridges fill the screen as far as the eye can see. A wind whips particles of snow up from the ground. 8.30 am.

Elspeth, small in the distance, struggles across the field, head down, fighting the wind. The blown snow stings her cheeks. The only sound is her breathing. She hugs her fur coat round her.

There's an ageless beauty in Elspeth; without make-up, hair blowing in the wind, sixty-three years old. She is as she is. The beauty's in her eyes.

EXT. THE CLIFF. MORNING

The cliff's in front of Elspeth. She goes along the path at its very edge.

A seagull cries, rises on the wind high above her.

TITLES

EXT. THE BANK. MORNING

The cliff path dips down a steep bank, pretty in summer but bleak now and covered in ice. Elspeth sidesteps down the slope very, very carefully.

EXT. THE BEACH. MORNING

It's a relief to reach the beach. The sand's hard. Snow in the crevices of the rocks. There's shelter from the wind. Walking's easier.

EXT. THE WALKWAY. MORNING

More shelter between the grey walls of the narrow walkway that leads up from the beach to the first houses of the little fishing village.

EXT. THE PEBBLE-DASH HOUSE. MORNING

Past a pebble-dash wall. The wind catches Elspeth. Takes her breath away. She grabs on to a pole. Fights to catch her breath. Her eyes close. She leans against the pole.

A council truck lumbers down the narrow road past the house. Too close. Loud in the silence. It startles her, brings her back to herself.

She makes herself walk on through a triangle of washing hanging frozen, strung between poles.

EXT. THE SLIPWAY/THE PROM. MORNING

She crosses the slipway. The prom's ahead of her.

Behind Elspeth the small seaside town comes to life. A curtain opens. A couple of workmen head for the bakery.

EXT. THE PROM. MORNING

Suddenly Elspeth skids on a patch of ice. She reaches out for the prom rail.

CUT TO:

INT. FRANCES'S BEDROOM. MORNING

Frances's fingers curl around the bed rail. She's deep in uneasy morning dreams. The kind of dreams, just on the edge of waking, that mix with memory and seem more real than life itself.

CUT TO:

EXT. THE ICE. MORNING

A seagull skids as it lands on a frozen pool. Mirror-like, the ice reflects the rocks and the wind-blown clouds in the sky.

CUT TO:

EXT. THE HOUSE BEACH. MORNING

Tom's hand picks up a stone from the beach. He's twelve years old. The white house rises up out of the rocks behind him. He flings the stone. It bounces off an old oil can. Scares the seagull. The bird rises up into the air screaming.

A squalling flock of gulls flies up from the ice to join it.

CUT TO:

INT. FRANCES'S BEDROOM. MORNING

Frances, thirty-six, turning over in bed, pulling the white duvet over her ears.

CUT TO:

EXT. FRANCES'S BACKYARD. MORNING

Alex, fifteen, coming out of his back door. He's carrying a black plastic rubbish bag out to the dustbin. The backyard has high whitewashed walls. It's cold, cold, cold. His jumper sleeves are pulled down over his hands. He looks up at the bird screeching overhead.

CUT TO:

EXT. SEAGULL'S POV. THE TOWN. MORNING

Tom's very small in the landscape. Shoulder hunched against the wind. His feet slip on icy rocks. The light's harsh.

The seagull's blown fast towards the town over the stark walls that protect the buildings from the sea. The long wharves reach out, grey against the sky. The town's exposed on its hillside; the promenade, the bus terminus, jagged grey-stone houses, narrow purple-shadowed lanes. Patches of snow in drifts in the crevices of the rocks on the beach. The seagull hovers, turns in the wind. There's the sea. Endless and still. And frozen.

EXT. THE PROM. MORNING

Elspeth holds the prom rail, looks up at the bird. Smiles.

TITLES END

EXT. THE SKY. MORNING

The seagull flies up and up. A small cottage perches on the hill above the white houses of the old harbour. A poor cottage. The paint's peeling. The windows are bare of curtains. The bird hurtles towards it.

CUT TO:

EXT. THE COTTAGE. MORNING

The seagull lands on the roof shrieking.

The sound of a baby crying.

CUT TO:

EXT. LOFT WINDOW. COTTAGE. MORNING

Nita's pressed against the glass, looking out at the birds. She's as wild as they are. Dark-haired and white-skinned. Sixteen years old. Waiting for life to come and get her.

CUT TO:

INT. THE KITCHEN. COTTAGE. MORNING

Nita's mother pushes food at the baby's mouth. A three-year-old slurps cocoa. The kitchen's a mess. The baby's a mess.

Nita comes to the table. Puts her arms round her mother's neck. Gives her a farewell kiss. There's obvious affection between them.

4

NITA'S MOTHER
Don't get too cold.

The baby's fat grabbing hands smear mushed food on the table.

CUT TO:

EXT. NITA'S FRONT DOOR. THE COTTAGE. MORNING

Nita bangs the door behind her. It rattles on the latch.

The world's wild around Nita. It's a relief to be free of the hot kitchen.

Her eye flicks to Alex's yard, looking for him.

CUT TO:

EXT. NITA'S POV. ALEX'S YARD. MORNING

He's dumping the garbage in the dustbin.

EXT. NITA'S GARDEN. MORNING

She runs down to the rail at the bottom of her garden. She tries desperately to keep Alex in view.

EXT. NITA'S POV. THE YARD. FRANCES'S HOUSE. MORNING

He's hauling the metal dustbin across the concrete. Half lifting, half dragging it to the yard gate.

EXT. THE SHED. MORNING

Nita whisks round and up over a wall on to the roof of a breeze-block shed. She can just see Alex.

Jumps down from the breeze-block shed and along the cliff path to the rail at the end. She leans out on the rail. Alex disappears into the street. The metal burns cold on her bare hand. She snatches it away and runs on.

CUT TO:

5

EXT. FRANCES'S HOUSE. MORNING

Alex leaves the dustbin at the front. Other dustbins in the square of white buildings on the harbour wait hopefully. He turns back to the house. Disappears in the back gate.

CUT TO:

EXT. FRANCES'S HOUSE. MORNING

Nita rounds the corner as the back gate closes. She runs down to the house railings, pausing a moment.

EXT. THE CUT. MORNING

She runs down the cut between the white houses on to the rocks and the beach. The wind hits her.

EXT. THE WALL. MORNING

The wall of Alex's backyard rises up high, straight out of the rocks. Nita scrambles over the rocks hugging close to the wall. She sneaks a look into the yard.

CUT TO:

EXT. THE BACKYARD. MORNING

Alex goes in the back door. Shuts it.

CUT TO:

EXT. THE HOUSE BEACH. MORNING

Nita leans, back to the wall, panting for breath.

Along the beach on a rock promontory Tom gazes out to sea. Ice glints from the rocks. The sun gleams through a crevice.

CUT TO:

INT. FRANCES'S BEDROOM. MORNING

The sunlight finds a gap in the blind. Plays with the dust motes. Touches the painted iron bed.

6

It's too large for one person. One side's untouched; pillows perfect.

The light's in Frances's eyes. She wakes with a cry for the dream she's lost.

CUT TO:

INT. THE KITCHEN/STAIRS. MORNING

Alex listening. He stops trying to find something to eat. The top's off the bread crock. The fridge is open. Calls.

ALEX

Are you all right?

CUT TO:

INT. FRANCES'S BEDROOM. MORNING

Frances sliding out of bed.

FRANCES

Don't keep asking.

She crosses the chaos of the bedroom. Books and photographs are piled on the floor. The wardrobe door's slightly open. Still, it's an attractive room, high-ceilinged and airy. There are line drawings on the walls.

7

*Frances pulls at the blind cord. Her wedding ring's loose on the hand
that rattles up the blind. The light shines in.*

CUT TO:

EXT. SCHOOL WYND. MORNING

*Two spry black-clad figures walk arm in arm down the steep walled
lane. Lily's tightly gloved hand touches lightly on the black handrail
bolted to the wall. Lily's sixty-five and smart as smart can be. Chloe's
sixty-eight. Her black has a rusty tinge to it. A raddled fox fur lies
round her neck. Her hand strays to it, stroking it now and then.*

*School Wynd opens out on to the town's main street. Carefully, oh so
carefully, Chloe and Lily cross the road to the prom.*

*Elspeth's a lone figure in the distance walking towards Frances's house.
Lily stares at her, receding.*

Elspeth walks on towards Frances's house.

                           LILY
        Not long for this world.

CHLOE

You can't tell that. Not just by looking.

LILY

Can I not?

CHLOE

D'you see a bus?

LILY

Your hem's down.

CHLOE

Eh?

She stops where she is by the high prom wall, bends, fiddles with the hem of her coat. Lily waits.

CUT TO:

EXT. THE HOUSE BEACH. MORNING

Nita's in among the rocks, crouched down with her back against the wall, blowing on her hands to warm them. Waiting. Listening.

CUT TO:

INT. THE LANDING/THE STAIRS. MORNING

Alex picks up matches from beside an oil lamp on the window seat. Shakes the box to see that it's not empty.

ALEX

Why don't you get the heating fixed?

He runs on up the stairs to the top landing; opens up the boiler cupboard.

INT. ALEX'S POV. FRANCES'S BEDROOM. MORNING

Frances stands at her bedroom window staring out. The sight of her standing there against the light stops Alex. Her short hair makes her look vulnerable. The whole lonely expanse of rock and sea and sky is beyond her through the window.

ALEX

Mum?

Frances starts into life. Swirls on her dressing-gown, pulls on thick socks.

FRANCES

You'll be late.

She begins to change the bed. Pulls covers off. Takes fresh sheets from the linen chest. The flying bed linen obscures her.

INT. THE TOP LANDING. MORNING

Alex pushes the plunger on the boiler that on a good day might ignite the pilot.

It clangs.

ALEX

Piece of crap, this.

FRANCES
(*off*)

Leave it.

ALEX

It's bloody freezing.

He leans in the doorway watching her.

FRANCES

I'm all right, Alex.

She doesn't look all right. She looks lost and hurt.

ALEX

I've left the immerser on.

He's reluctant to leave her. She smiles at him.

FRANCES

I don't need a nursemaid.

INT. THE STAIRS. MORNING

Alex bounds down the bare polished-wood stairs past piles of black and white photographs. They're all of Jamie, Alex's father. Most are unframed. They blur in and out of focus as he rushes past.

CUT TO:

EXT. THE PROM WALL. MORNING

Chloe's bent double by the prom wall trying to pin up her hem.

Lily's sighing at the delay.

> CHLOE
> More hurry less speed.

> LILY
> I'm not missing this. It's a young one. I haven't been to a young funeral since I don't know when.

> CHLOE
> April.

> LILY
> Eh?

> CHLOE
> His. His from the old harbour.

Frances's house is far in the distance.

> LILY
> (*voice-over*)
> Wasn't that young.

CUT TO:

INT. THE HALL. MORNING

> CHLOE
> (*voice-over*)
> Forty, Lily. Young to you and me.

Photographs of Jamie line the mantelpiece. Alex is putting on his blazer at the mirror over the fireplace. There are two cameras on the oak table behind him. And books and more books.

CUT TO:

EXT. THE PROM WALL. MORNING

Lily snatches the hem and the pin away from Chloe.

> LILY
>
> You're like a cow with a musket.

> CHLOE
>
> He was a very handsome man.

> LILY
>
> They pop their clogs to spite you.

> CHLOE
>
> Eh?

> LILY
>
> I'm glad I never married.

Lily sees the longing in Chloe's face.

The pin jabs Chloe in the leg.

> CHLOE
>
> Lily!

Her hand goes down to rub the sore place.

    CUT TO:

EXT. THE HOUSE BEACH. MORNING.

Nita sneaks a look into the backyard just as Alex comes out the back door. He's almost coming towards her. She ducks and runs away, slithering on the glassy surface of the rocks.

EXT. THE WHARF. MORNING

Nita climbs the wharf wall. Runs down the wharf itself, across the front of Frances's house and away passing Elspeth by the old harbour.

    CUT TO:

EXT. THE BACKYARD. MORNING

Alex takes his bike out of the shed. He leans it against the yard wall. Clamps his hands in his armpits to keep them warm.

He's watching the house.

    CUT TO:

INT. THE BEDROOM. MORNING

Frances leafing through a pile of architectural photographs.

She comes across a forgotten photograph of Jamie. Runs her finger down the jaw line and the throat.

    CUT TO:

EXT. THE OLD HARBOUR/THE RAILED PATH. MORNING

Elspeth crosses the road to Frances's house. She leans on the iron gate. Catches her breath. The walk's taken a lot out of her. More than it should have. She has to fight to retain consciousness.

She walks up the railed path to the backyard gate. Her hand's on the house wall for balance.

    CUT TO:

EXT. FRANCES'S YARD. MORNING

Alex hears his grandmother struggle with the latch. He tries to hide by the shed, knocks the bike over. The gate opens.

ELSPETH

What are you still here for?

Her voice bites. Her back straightens. She won't let her grandson see any sign of weakness.

ALEX

I didn't know you were coming.

ELSPETH

Well, you know now.

He looks up at the back of the house.

Go to school, cherub.

As Alex wheels his bike past his grandmother, he kisses her. Takes a last glance up at the house.

You leave her to me. Go on.

Alex goes. Elspeth watches him.

CUT TO:

EXT. THE OLD HARBOUR. MORNING

Nita runs in between stacks of fish crates and trailing orange nets. Seagulls peck at remains.

EXT. THE FISH MARKET. MORNING

Nita runs through the arches of the fish market. Her footsteps echo in the great empty space. She keeps on running out the other side and down the slipway to the town beach.

CUT TO:

EXT. FRANCES'S YARD. MORNING

Elspeth unlocks the back door. Calls.

                    ELSPETH
Frances?

CUT TO:

INT. THE BEDROOM/THE BATHROOM. MORNING

Frances starts at the sound of her mother's voice. She slides along the hall into the bathroom. Shuts the door very quietly.

CUT TO:

INT. FRANCES'S KITCHEN. MORNING

Elspeth putting the butter in the fridge.

                    ELSPETH
Frances?

She listens.

CUT TO:

16

INT. THE BATHROOM. MORNING

Frances has her back to the bathroom door. She's not ready to face her mother.

> ELSPETH
> *(off)*
> Are you all right, cherub?

Frances turns on the taps. Water and steam gush out.

CUT TO:

EXT. THE TOWN BEACH. MORNING

Nita rolling snow into a snowman shape. She's looking up from the beach. Keeping an eye out for Alex. Her hands are red cold.

CUT TO:

INT. THE KITCHEN. MORNING

Elspeth shivering. She touches a cold radiator.

> ELSPETH
> Ttt, tt, tt.

Doesn't take off her coat.

Goes past the empty grate in the breakfast room. Picks up a jumper from the floor. Hears the sound of running water from the bathroom.

CUT TO:

EXT. THE RAILED PATH/THE HILL. MORNING

Alex wheels his bike down the railed path at the side of the house. The wind's against him.

A Woman's walking down the hill above him with two children strapped into a double buggy and one hanging on to a handle. He slips. The Woman yanks him to his feet.

WOMAN

Need a pair of skates, eh?

Alex smiles; pushes the bike across the harbour road.

CUT TO:

INT. THE STAIRS. MORNING

Elspeth climbing the stairs to the landing. Hand gripping the banister. Decides not to knock on the bathroom door. One of the photographs is very clear beside her.

ELSPETH

Don't you look at me like that.

She turns the photograph to the wall.

There. Serves you right.

Puts her hand on the telescope.

CUT TO:

INT. FRANCES'S HOUSE. MORNING

Elspeth looks through the telescope.

Sees Alex walking with the bike along the harbour road.

Sees Chloe and Lily on the other side by the wall.

CUT TO:

EXT. THE PROM. MORNING

Chloe and Lily walk towards the bus shelter.

CHLOE

Cream?

LILY

There wasn't any.

CHLOE

Och, your face and parsley.

Did you have a fridge?

CHLOE

Did we have a fridge?

LILY

No fridge, no cream.

A Man slips as he passes them.

Lily draws back out of the way.

MAN

I beg your pardon.

LILY

That's quite all right.

Lily smiles a little pursed-mouth smile. The wind blows. Chloe glares at her.

CUT TO:

INT. THE LANDING. MORNING

Elspeth focusing the telescope on the fur round Chloe's neck.

ELSPETH

Call that fox?

The dead eye on the fox fur's dull.

CUT TO:

EXT. THE BUS SHELTER. MORNING.

ELSPETH
(*voice-over*)

Dyed rabbit. Died long ago that. Wants burying, that's what that wants.

Bright sun shines on the black-clad ladies as they reach the bus shelter.

Lily dusts off the bench. Sits.

Chloe neck craning, dewlap, slides round the side of the shelter. Looks for a bus.

> ELSPETH
> (*voice-over*)
> Bury her with it. Best thing.

CUT TO:

INT. THE LANDING. MORNING

> ELSPETH
> Face on her. What's she done to get a face like that?

CUT TO:

EXT. THE BUS STOP. MORNING

Lily opens up a too-big newspaper.

> LILY
> You need a refrigerator for cream, Chloe. And that's a fact.

> CHLOE
> I'll tell you what you need for cream, Lily. You need a cow for cream, Lily.

> LILY
> Eh?

> CHLOE
> A cow, Lily!

> LILY
> I'm always glad to learn something, Chloe.

The newspaper rattles.

> CHLOE
> My mother used to make trifles.

Chloe's walking up and down to keep warm.

> LILY
> Your mother's trifles!

CHLOE

What?

LILY

Custard.

CHLOE

Custard?

LILY

Custard permeated your house, Chloe, the smell of it.
Curtains minging with it. Pears in custard. Apple pie. Your
mother? Custard in the trifles!

CHLOE

Thick cream!

The newspaper rattles.

Whipped cream! And I remember the fork that she whipped it
with.

LILY

1956. That's when there was cream. I remember a meringue
in Jenners's tea room.

CHLOE

You had milk, I suppose?

LILY

Eh?

CHLOE

You drank milk.

LILY

Of course we drank milk, Chloe. Don't be so damn stupid.

CHLOE

And where did you keep it?

LILY

In a brown clay jug, in the larder, all wrapped around with a
cold wet cloth.

CHLOE

And that's where you kept the cream. In a smaller jug right by its very side. I'm telling you.

CUT TO:

EXT. THE HOUSE BEACH. MORNING

Tom's standing looking out at the frozen sea. He's fascinated by it.

Sam's creeping up on Tom. He's twelve, the same age as Tom but there's an energy about Sam; a confidence that Tom lacks.

Sam leaps on Tom, gets a stranglehold on him.

TOM

Get off.

SAM

I put the pressure on. I put the pressure on here.

He's pressing against the bone behind Tom's ear.

Feel that eh? Feel it?

TOM

I feel it. I feel it.

SAM

Know what this is called. Eh? Eh?

TOM

No.

SAM

I can't hear you.

TOM

I don't know what it's fucking called.

SAM

Want to know?

TOM

You're hurting me.

SAM

Do you want to know what this is called?

TOM

Yes. Yes.

SAM

A 'Killer', this is called. A fucking 'Killer'.

TOM

Get off! Get off!

SAM

I squeeze, that's all. Five seconds and you're dead. Feel that?

Silence.

Do you feel that?

TOM
(*yelling at the top of his voice*)

I fucking feel it.

SAM

I'm counting. One Two.

Fuck off.

He kicks hard at Sam's legs.

EXT. THE WHARF. MORNING

They race up over the wharf wall. Round the side of Frances's house over to the corner of the old harbour where there's the chained and padlocked roundabout of rotten wood and two ancient rusty prom horses.

Sam leaps on to a horse. Dumps his rucksack in the snow.

SAM

Race you.

TOM

Eh?

Sam gets the horse going.

SAM

First one to touch.

TOM

Fucking cheat you.

He clambers on to his horse.

The creak of prom horses fills the cold morning. The sun gleams bright.

In the distance Lily looks up from her paper.

CHLOE

They want oiled.

LILY

Put down. That's what they want. Gun to the head. Kindest in the long run.

CUT TO:

INT. THE FRONT ROOM. FRANCES'S HOUSE. MORNING

Elspeth opening the front-room curtains. She sees the boys across the road. The creaking of the horses is faint.

Elspeth mutters to herself.

ELSPETH

Boys!

She smiles at their antics.

CUT TO:

EXT. THE BUS SHELTER. MORNING

The boys are working and working the horses.

Chloe shivers watching Sam and Tom.

LILY

Have you not got your vest on?

CHLOE

A goose walked over my grave.

LILY

Don't say that. I hate it when you say that.

CHLOE

They should be in school.

LILY

Do you see a bus?

CHLOE

Eh?

LILY

How do you propose they get there?

CHLOE

Once before I've seen the sea frozen. Long, long ago. Only
the once. The day that was.

There's a soft look on Chloe's face that Lily can't abide.

LILY

What are you talking about?

Chloe won't tell.

Cuts through you that wind. Cuts you in two.

She bites her lips as she watches the boys. The sound of a distant piano.

CUT TO:

INT. THE FRONT ROOM. FRANCES'S HOUSE. MORNING

Elspeth holding back the front-room curtains. Watching the boys race. The creaking's faint.

The piano's softer in the house, on the edge of hearing; a bored piano, playing the same tune over and over.

ELSPETH
Red cheeks. Monkeys.

CUT TO:

EXT. THE HORSES. MORNING

The horses are rocking wildly.

SAM
Touching.

Still working them.

TOM
Bloody isn't.

SAM
Bloody touching.

TOM
It's not bloody touching.

Sam stands on his horse's back. Whacks his foot down. His horse's tail digs into the ice.

Wanker.

Sam leaps on to Tom's horse, making it tip backwards. Jumps down and runs. The horse lurches forward. Tom lurches with it. Just lands on

26

*his knees on the ice. There's a hole in his trousers. His knee's bleeding.
He licks it. Sam's far away.*

Come here you, Sam. You.

*Tom runs along the prom road on to the new harbour wharf, through
the fish crates to the oil tanks, chasing Sam. Limping. He's easily
outdistanced.*

They creak, the horses. To and fro. To and fro.

The sound of the distant piano.

CUT TO:

INT. THE BATHROOM. FRANCES'S HOUSE. MORNING

*Frances in the bath watching a drop of condensation run down the
mirror. The piano's softer in the bathroom. Her hair's slick with water.
The boiler plunger begins to clang.*

CUT TO:

INT. THE BOILER CUPBOARD. FRANCES'S HOUSE. MORNING

*Elspeth pushing and pushing the plunger. Nothing ignites. She gives up.
Hugs her coat round her. Nearly knocks on the bathroom door.*

*Hears the tune that's being played on the piano. Calls through to the
bathroom.*

> ELSPETH
> There's someone at the piano, cherub. Can you hear?
> (*sings*)
> O can ye wash a sailor's shirt.
> O can ye wash it clean.

CUT TO:

INT. THE BATHROOM. FRANCES'S HOUSE. MORNING

*Frances sinking under the water in the steam-filled bathroom, trying to
cut out her mother's voice.*

ELSPETH
(*off; singing*)
O can ye wash a sailor's shirt
And hang it on the green.

CUT TO:

INT. THE BATHROOM DOOR. FRANCES'S HOUSE. MORNING

ELSPETH
(*listening*)
Summer music that.

(*waiting for a reply*)
Frances!

CUT TO:

INT. THE BATHROOM. FRANCES'S HOUSE. MORNING

Frances emerging from the water. Grabbing a towel. Getting out of the bath.

ELSPETH
(*off*)
Boarding house music.

Frances wipes a circle of mirror clear of steam. She mouths her own name in the mirror as:

Frances?

CUT TO:

INT. THE BATHROOM DOOR. FRANCES'S HOUSE. MORNING

Elspeth's worried by the silence.

ELSPETH
D'you remember Prestwick, cherub? And the food in that place. 'The Farmer's Boy' we had over and over.
(*sings*)
. . . to be a Farmer's boy.

The words slide away from her. Sings:

Thing thing thing.

Elspeth looks very frail. She has to grip on to the banister. Her breath comes fast. She closes her eyes. Silence.

CUT TO:

INT. THE BATHROOM. FRANCES'S HOUSE. MORNING

Frances listens to the stillness.

> ELSPETH
> (*off*)
> They stuffed you. The food.

Frances's relieved when her mother speaks.

CUT TO:

INT. THE LANDING. MORNING

Elspeth's hand is white on the banister. Speaking's an effort.

> ELSPETH
> You couldn't move.

CUT TO:

EXT. MENZIES' WINDOW. MORNING

> ELSPETH
> (*voice-over*)
> We were all sick when we got back that year. D'you remember that, cherub?

Trays of pies lie in the steamed-up window. Alex's bike leans against it. Through the steam, inside the shop, the Menzies lady slips a mutton pie into a paper bag and hands it to Alex across the counter.

CUT TO:

INT. THE STAIRS. FRANCES'S HOUSE. MORNING

Elspeth sinks down on to a stair, leans against the spindles.

ELSPETH
And the tide come galloping in.

Her breathing slows. She opens her eyes.

Cherub? Frances?

FRANCES
(*off*)
I'm washing my hair.

ELSPETH
And the beauty competition. Oh, Frances. Miss Prestwick
Junior. I was proud.

CUT TO:

INT. THE BATHROOM. FRANCES'S HOUSE. MORNING

*Relief turns to exasperation. Frances turns the tap on in the sink to
drown out her mother's voice.*

ELSPETH
(*off*)
Your round wee tummy and your round wee bottom. Wiggle
waggle wiggle waggling.

Frances can still hear. She puts her hands over her ears.

CUT TO:

INT. THE LANDING. FRANCES'S HOUSE. MORNING

Elspeth smiles.

ELSPETH
Walking round the swimming-pool for all the world to see.

*She pulls herself to her feet. Picks up a sweatshirt. Walks through to
Alex's bedroom.*

Parading.

CUT TO:

INT. BATHROOM FRANCES'S HOUSE. MORNING

Frances sinks down on to the bathroom floor, hands tight over her ears. Tap running. Listening.

> ELSPETH
> (*off*)
> In your bubbly red swimming-suit and your hair all the way to your wee fat bottom.

Frances tugs at her urchin-short hair, half wet, half dry.

> I could've run down there; I could have bitten it for you, that bottom.

Frances stares at the coloured motes of light shining through the stained glass at the window.

CUT TO:

INT. ALEX'S BEDROOM. FRANCES'S HOUSE. MORNING

> ELSPETH
> A good hard bite. And the lovely smile on your face.

Elspeth catches sight of herself in Alex's mirror. What she sees doesn't please her.

CUT TO:

EXT. THE TOWN BEACH. MORNING

> ELSPETH
> (*voice-over*)
> And all the folk looking.

Nita looks up from making her snowman. She checks to see if Alex is on the prom. Doesn't find him. Picks up a shell.

> I knew. I knew then that you were blest in all the world.

CUT TO:

EXT. THE MAIN ROAD. MORNING

Alex wheels his bike along the main road. Bites into his pie. Crosses to the prom side.

ELSPETH
(*voice-over*)
Lucky for life, and I was too that I had you.

CUT TO:

INT. ALEX'S BEDROOM. MORNING

Elspeth puts the sweatshirt down on a chest of drawers.

ELSPETH
Lucky Frances.

Murmurs.

Touch wood when you say that.

She does.

Throw salt over your shoulder.
(*sings*)
O can ye wash a sailor's shirt.

CUT TO:

INT. THE BATHROOM. FRANCES'S HOUSE. MORNING

Silence. Frances listening. She doesn't like the talk. She likes the silence less.

FRANCES
I can't hear you.

CUT TO:

INT. ALEX'S BEDROOM/LANDING. FRANCES'S HOUSE. MORNING

ELSPETH
And your picture in the paper.

Her voice is very low. Dreaming. Lost. She walks down to the landing window.

I have it. I have it yet. Don't you worry.

She listens to the silence.

What is it, cherub?

No reply.

Frances?

CUT TO:

INT. THE BATHROOM. MORNING

Frances turns her head away.

CUT TO:

INT. THE LANDING. MORNING

Elspeth looks out of the window. Her face is bleak.

CUT TO:

EXT. ELSPETH'S POV. THE TOWN BEACH. MORNING

Far, far away Nita's working at her snowman.

CUT TO:

EXT. THE TOWN BEACH/MENZIES. MORNING

The sun glares off the snow. Nita's carving her snowman's face with a razor shell. He's a fine snowman.

She shades her eyes with her hand.

Alex crosses the road munching. Rests his bike against the prom rail. He doesn't even glance in Nita's direction.

She picks up a handful of snow. Shapes a snowball.

Alex leans, bites into a mince pie half sticking out of a paper bag saying 'MENZIES'.

Nita throws the snowball. Turns an innocent back.

The snowball's right on target. Alex's pie flies out of his hand, splats down on to the ice. The mince spills out. The bag blows away. Alex looks for a culprit. Finally sees Nita.

ALEX

D'you throw that?

NITA

What?

ALEX

Snowball.

NITA

What?

ALEX

That's my pie.

NITA

Was it a Menzies one?

ALEX

It was my breakfast.

NITA

Carmichael's make better pies.

ALEX

Eh?

NITA

Carmichael's.

ALEX

Right you are. Thank you. Next time I want to buy a pie to chuck on the pavement I'll be sure and get it from Carmichael's.

Alex mounts his bike.

Nita runs to the prom rail. Hand down on the rock to steady herself.

The bike bumps awkwardly on the pitted ice. The chain comes off. Alex's feet go round and round on nothing. The bike tips. Alex leaps. The bike falls. Alex falls.

CUT TO:

34

INT. ELSPETH'S POV. THE LANDING WINDOW. MORNING

ELSPETH

Oh my God.

Her hand's at her mouth.

Nita's laughing.

CUT TO:

EXT. THE PROM. MORNING.

Alex rubbing his elbow.

ALEX

Shit!

NITA

Are you all right?

Nita climbs over the prom rail.

ALEX

What do you care?

Alex stands the bike on its saddle.

Nita watches him fiddle.

NITA

Want a hand?

ALEX

I'm fine.

Nita kneels beside him.

The chain's covering his hands in oil.

NITA

Here.

She loops the chain on.

Small cog first.

She grins up at him. Face lifted in the sun. He stares at her.

CUT TO:

INT. ELSPETH'S POV. THE LANDING WINDOW. MORNING

Elspeth's peering through the telescope.

ELSPETH

You be careful, Alex.

The telescope's fixed on Nita.

It wants that face.

CUT TO:

EXT. THE PROM. MORNING

Nita's concentrating. Fixing the chain on to the large cog.

ELSPETH
(voice-over)

Give her the moon, she'd want the stars as well.

CUT TO:

INT. THE LANDING WINDOW. FRANCES'S HOUSE. MORNING

Elspeth wipes her eyes with her handkerchief.

ELSPETH

Ah, we all want. I want. I've always wanted. I'm wanting yet.

CUT TO:

EXT. THE PROM. MORNING

ALEX

I can fix my own chain.

NITA

Oh well.

She starts to take it off again.

ALEX

Don't take it off. Hey!

NITA

You can fix it, you said.

ALEX

Leave the bloody thing.

He catches her hand.

I said leave it. What's your name?

NITA

Nita.

ALEX

Eh?

NITA

Nita, for God's sake.

Alex stares at her.

You've got my hand.

ALEX

Nita?

CUT TO:

INT. THE LANDING. FRANCES'S HOUSE. DAY

Elspeth sliding away from the window. Calls to Frances on her way through the hall into Frances's bedroom.

>   ELSPETH
> I'll make the bed, cherub.

CUT TO:

EXT. THE PROM. MORNING

>   NITA
> You've still got my hand.

She's grinning at him. He lets go.

CUT TO:

INT. THE BATHROOM. FRANCES'S HOUSE. MORNING

Frances hasn't moved from the floor.

>   ELSPETH
>   (*off*)
> I'm making your bed for you.

CUT TO:

EXT. THE PROM. MORNING

Nita slides through the prom rails on to the beach. The sound of a piano. Alex waits to see if she'll look back. She doesn't.

Then she does. But he's gone, wheeling the bike off up Bruce's Wynd.

CUT TO:

EXT. THE FAR WHARF. MORNING

Tom's up on the sea wall. Caught by the glitter of the ice.

CUT TO:

EXT. THE FISH CRATES. MORNING

Sam's holding a scabby piece of fish out to a seagull. The seagull eyes him. The piano just reaches Sam. He turns his head. The seagull lunges. Takes the fish. Nips Sam's fingers.

SAM

Away tae fuck.

He shakes his hand to get the pain away.

Bastard.

The seagull swallows the fish.

CUT TO:

EXT. THE PUBLIC CONVENIENCE. MORNING

Chloe rattles the door but it's padlocked.

CUT TO:

EXT. THE BUS STOP. MORNING

Lily stops reading the paper. Lifts her head and listens to the piano.

CUT TO:

INT. FRANCES'S BATHROOM. MORNING

The piano's loud in the bathroom.

Frances listens. Reaches up and turns off the taps.

CUT TO:

INT. FRANCES'S BEDROOM. MORNING

Elspeth leans on the rail of the painted iron bedstead.

ELSPETH

Listen, Frances. Listen, cherub. D'you hear that?

It's 'Vair Me Oh' on the piano.

                          (sings)
Thou'rt the music of my heart.
Harp of joy oh cruish moh cridh

She goes on singing.

CUT TO:

EXT. THE BUS SHELTER. MORNING

A whisper of an image of Elspeth holding on to the bedpost singing softly.

                        ELSPETH
                      (voice-over)
Moon of guidance by night
La, la, la
La, la, la . . .

As Lily shakes her paper.

And Chloe walks back.

                       CHLOE
There's no bus coming. There's none in sight.

She shivers.

                      LILY
What's wrong with you?

                       CHLOE
I'm cold, that's all.

                      LILY
Stamp your feet then.

                       CHLOE
I need the toilet.

                      LILY
Cross your legs.

                       CHLOE
I'm not a contortionist, Lily.

The piano plays. Elspeth sings.

INT. FRANCES'S BEDROOM. MORNING

Elspeth listening to the piano; singing under her breath.

> CHLOE
> (*voice-over*)
> Catch your death standing here. Catch your death before you catch a bus.

CUT TO:

EXT. THE BUS SHELTER. MORNING

Chloe nods at the newspaper.

> CHLOE
> Anyone we know?

> LILY
> No. No, I don't think so. Not yet.

Chloe draws her coat around her.

CUT TO:

INT. FRANCES'S BEDROOM. MORNING

The piano stops.

> ELSPETH
> There. Pity.

She smooths the bedcover.

CUT TO:

INT. THE BATHROOM. MORNING

There are tears on Frances's cheeks. She wipes them roughly away.

CUT TO:

EXT. THE BUS SHELTER. MORNING

Lily's rattling and rustling the newspaper.

LILY

Oh, Chloe.

A folding and a crackling.

CHLOE

What?

LILY

'Peacefully at home.'

CHLOE

Who?

LILY

Guess.

CHLOE

Guess?

LILY

Go on, Chloe.

CHLOE

Tell me.

Chloe peers over Lily's shoulder. Lily hides the paper from Chloe.

LILY

'Will be remembered.' What will she be remembered for? Eh?
You answer me that.

CHLOE

That's my paper.

She grabs at it.

LILY

Ah ah ah.

CHLOE

Give it to me.

LILY

Don't be a spoilsport. A wee bit fun, Chloe. Guess. Go on,
Chloe. Please.

(*pause*)

CHLOE

Do I get the age?

LILY

A February birthday, I'll give you that.

CHLOE

Aquarius.

LILY

A February birthday, a February death. Nice and round.

CHLOE

I don't know who it was.

Chloe snatches the paper.

Where? Where is it?

LILY

There.

She takes off her glasses and passes them to Chloe.

CHLOE

Well, well, well, well, well.
(*pause*)
She'll be remembered. I'll say she'll be remembered.

LILY

Last saw her in Skinners. Eating a chocolate meringue.

CHLOE

This cold'll take a few.

LILY

So it will.

CHLOE

We'll be spoilt for choice.

LILY

Funeral's on Thursday. Are we free?

They check their diaries.

CHLOE

Today we've got. Wednesday we've got.

LILY

We'll mark Thursday in then.
                                                    (*reads*)
'No flowers.'

CHLOE

Pity. I like a nice floral tribute. No one thinks of the mourners.

CUT TO:

EXT. THE WHARF WALL. MORNING

Tom staring out at a dazzle of light. Sun on ice. Turns at Sam's arrival.

TOM

Fucking brilliant, eh?

SAM

Wanker.

Tom hits out. Sam dodges. Runs.

EXT. THE WHARF. MORNING

Tom chases Sam all the way along the wharf to the prom.

EXT. THE TOWN BEACH. MORNING

Sam jumps down on to the town beach.

Tom leaps on Sam. Sam's laughing. The boys roll.

They bump into Nita. Knock her into the snowman. It's wrecked. Sam runs.

NITA

You wee sods look what you've bloody well done.

She runs. Cuts Sam off. Catches hold of him.

SAM

Wasnie me, it was him. You blind, are you?

TOM

Fuck off, Sam.

Sam gets away from Nita.

NITA

You better run.

SAM

What're you gonnie do?

NITA

I'm gonnie murder you, you wee bugger.

SAM

Don't you touch me.

NITA

Come on, come here.

SAM

Keep your fucking hands to yourself.

NITA

Look at the big man.

SAM

Think I'm feart, do you?

TOM

Come on, Sam.

SAM

I'm not scared of you.

Tom grabs Sam.

TOM

Leave it, hey. Come on. Come on, Sam.

45

Sam and Tom are running along the beach.

Nita's chasing the boys. She falls. Hands grab her. Pull her to her feet.

ALEX

It's a snowman. That's all.

NITA

It's my snowman.

ALEX

Leave them alone.

Alex is still holding her. The boys are running away, far on up the beach they go, and out of sight.

NITA

I wanted him perfect.

ALEX

Doesn't matter.

NITA

I thought you'd gone.

ALEX

I came back.

NITA

What for?

It's an inviting look she gives him. He can't cope. He lets her go.

ALEX

You're all wet.

NITA

Come out on the ice with me.

ALEX

Five to nine. I should be in school.

NITA

Come out on the ice. Come on. Come on. Come out now. Won't wait.

ALEX

You daft or what are you?

She's very close to him.

NITA

Do you not want to know what it feels like?

ALEX

Eh?

He can't look at her.

NITA

What if there's only this day left to us? Out of all our lives this one day. Come out on the ice.

ALEX

We'll drown out there.

NITA

You can swim, can't you?

The wind blows her hair. She holds out her hand.

CUT TO:

INT. FRANCES'S BATHROOM. MORNING

Frances picking up the wet towels from the floor.

CUT TO:

EXT. THE BUS SHELTER. MORNING

Chloe's shivering, scluffing her feet and stamping them.

LILY

Suck on a peppermint.

CHLOE

Eh?

LILY

An Extra Strong Mint. Keep you warm.

CHLOE

Have you got one?

Lily searches in her bag.

CUT TO:

EXT. THE BEACH. MORNING

Alex taking Nita's hand.

CUT TO:

EXT. THE BUS STOP. MORNING

Lily snapping her bag shut.

LILY

I haven't.

CHLOE

You haven't got a peppermint?

LILY

I haven't.

CHLOE

Getting my hopes up. Think before you speak, Lily. I'll thank you to do that.

LILY

I'm sorry.

CHLOE

Easy enough said. Sorry. Doesn't make it better. The expectation. An Extra Strong Mint. I'm salivating.

A wind blows the snow. Chloe looks up at the driven clouds covering the sun. For a moment the cold's bitter.

LILY

Will we walk?

CHLOE

The old days with them walking in front. That's what I liked. The dancing days.

48

LILY

Hardly dancing. Hardly at funerals.

CHLOE

No such thing as funerals then. No one died then.

She looks across at the frozen sea.

CUT TO:

EXT. THE SEA'S EDGE. MORNING

The ice isn't clean at the sea's edge. There's a yellow tinge to it.

NITA

Feel the fear running up and down your back. Cold fingers
on your vertebrae.

ALEX

Come on.

*Hauls her up the beach. Pulls her fast down on to the ice. Stops. She's
laughing.*

Shhhhhhhhh!

Puts his finger on her lips.

Right. Right. Tiptoe.

They set out on to the ice, stepping very carefully.

CUT TO:

INT. FRANCES'S BATHROOM. MORNING

Frances makes herself open the bathroom door.

INT. BEDROOM. MORNING

*She sweeps across the hall and into the bedroom. Dumps the towels in
the dirty linen basket.*

ELSPETH

Oh my God.

49

She's looking at Frances's reflection. Frances's hand strays up. Tugs at her hair. Grabs leggings and socks. Yanks them on.

> **FRANCES**
> The man who led me round that pool was a ballocks. The bathing suit rubbed my nipples raw. The tops of my thighs got chapped on the elastic. My right nipple has a bit off the tip because of that bathing suit. When we got back to the boarding house we had egg for tea. You made me eat the white because of India's starving millions. And I spewed up. The boarding house woman was blazing because I didn't get to the bathroom and all the sick went down the cracks in the linoleum. You put me to bed and there was a thunderstorm. You have a very selective memory, Mother.

She pulls on a jumper.

> **ELSPETH**
> What have you done? What have you done to your hair?

Frances searches the dressing table for eye make-up. Can't find it.

INT. THE STAIRS. MORNING

Frances runs downstairs into the front room.

Elspeth follows.

> **ELSPETH**
> Oh, Frances. Your lovely hair. Cherub. What have you done?

> **FRANCES**
> Cut it.

> **ELSPETH**
> I can see that. That's plain to see.

The breath's gone out of her. She has to hang on to the banister. As the women move round the house, the argument flows on.

INT. THE FRONT ROOM. MORNING

Frances lifts cushions looking for her bag.

                        FRANCES
Needed a change.

                        ELSPETH
Oh God.

Finds her bag. Empties it out on the sofa. There's no make-up.

                        FRANCES
Don't you like it?

                        ELSPETH
Your beautiful hair.

INT. THE HALL. MORNING

Frances sweeps out into the hall.

                        FRANCES
A trim, that's all.

                        ELSPETH
Is that what you call it?

The make-up's on the mantelpiece among the photographs of Jamie.

                        FRANCES
It'll grow.

                        ELSPETH
Did you pay someone to do that to you?

Frances puts on eye make-up.

                        FRANCES
Boyish, don't you think?

                        ELSPETH
Mannish.

                        FRANCES
Gives me cheekbones.

                        ELSPETH
Doesn't make you look any younger.

FRANCES

The time has come for me to embrace my years, don't you think, Mother? Welcome them. Not fight them any more.

ELSPETH

Why should you embrace your years? No one else does. It's the kingdom of youth that we're living in, Frances. I never thought I'd see you let yourself go. No matter what's happened to you. Never give in. Is it your work?

FRANCES

Say something nice, Mother. Try.

ELSPETH

You've always had good bone structure. You get that from me. I'll make a beautiful skeleton when my time comes. Makes your neck longer. Very handsome.

FRANCES

Thank you.

Elspeth sits on the stairs.

ELSPETH

Have you kept it?

FRANCES

What?

ELSPETH

Your hair.

FRANCES

No.

ELSPETH

I mean, if you were going to a hot country.

Elspeth wants to be reassured. Frances won't look at her mother.

Didn't they give it to you?

FRANCES

I didn't ask.

ELSPETH

I'd've liked it. Did you never think of that? To keep. Did you never think of me? Of course you didn't. When have you ever, ever, ever thought of me? Maybe they've still got it.

FRANCES

Be in a wig by now.

ELSPETH

Have you been out like that?
(*pause*)
What does Alex say?

FRANCES

He likes it.

ELSPETH

He'd say that. He'd say that to keep you happy. You've taught that lad well.

Frances goes upstairs past her mother.

The photographs blur in and out of focus.

Wear some earrings, for God's sake. Let folk know you're a woman. Long earrings.

Frances shuts the bedroom door.

Are you going to Australia, Frances? Are you going to live there? Is that why you cut it?

Elspeth turns a photograph round.

I blame you for this. My God.

Elspeth walks to the window.

CUT TO:

EXT. THE FROZEN SEA. MORNING

Nita standing quite still, surrounded by ice. There's mist on the horizon.

NITA

We can get to the rock.

INT. FRANCES'S BEDROOM. MORNING

Frances pulling a jumper out of a chest. Slips the jumper on.

>   ALEX
>   (*voice-over*)
>   It's getting thinner . . .

>   NITA
>   (*voice-over*)
>   It's not.

>   ALEX
>   (*voice-over*)
>   Look at it.

CUT TO:

EXT. THE FROZEN SEA. MORNING

Breath puffs smokily in the air.

>   ALEX
>   For God's sake, Nita, you can practically see the fish.

>   NITA
>   You go back if you want.

She jumps from one rock to another.

>   ALEX
>   Christ.

He jumps after her, lands on the ice and goes straight through. Up to his ankles. Stands there rigid with cold.

>   Jesus.

Nita starts to laugh.

>   It isn't fucking funny, Nita.

He steps.

>   I could get frostbite.

The ice breaks.

I could get gangrene.

NITA

You've made a fishing hole.

ALEX

People get their limbs cut off. They lose their toes, Nita.

NITA

You're three metres from the beach.

Alex sees a maroon and white bus at the terminus.

ALEX

There's a bloody bus. They can all get to school Nita. Nita, for Christ's sake.

He steps on to solid ice. Walks gingerly back to the shore.

LILY
(*voice-over*)

Is that not a twenty-six?

CUT TO:

EXT. THE BUS STOP. MORNING

Lily's looking at the white top of the bus just visible at the terminus.

LILY

Will we run for it?

CHLOE

My running days are long gone.

LILY

You've a fine pair of legs on you.

CHLOE

Eh?

LILY

It's a big funeral this and I'm not missing it. I like a show.

CUT TO:

INT. BEDROOM. FRANCES'S HOUSE. DAY

Frances gathering all the architectural photographs. She doesn't touch the picture of Jamie.

CUT TO:

EXT. THE BUS SHELTER. MORNING

Lily folding the paper.

LILY
With or without you. That's my bus.

She crosses the road. Heels clicking on the ice.

CHLOE
Lily!

She nearly walks out into the road in the path of a scooter. The driver swerves to avoid her.

It's a narrow escape and it frightens her. A little rush of traffic cuts her off from Lily.

CUT TO:

EXT. THE SHORE. MORNING

Alex hopping about, taking off his shoes and socks.

NITA
You could sit down.

ALEX
Where do you come from?

NITA
I live up on the hill.

ALEX
That's nice for you. You'll have a sea view.

He glares at her.

NITA
Here.

56

She holds out her hand.

> ALEX
>
> Don't you bloody touch me.

> NITA
>
> Come on.

> ALEX
>
> Get away from me.

He falls over. In among the seaweed and the stones and the snow.

She's laughing at him.

He catches hold of her.

He pulls her down in the snow with him.

> That's for wrecking my breakfast.

> NITA
>
> I'll buy you another one.

He's holding a handful of snow over her.

> Don't, Alex.

He's rubbing snow on her face and in her hair.

> Aleeex!

He puts a handful down the neck of her sweatshirt. Soaks her.

> ALEX
>
> If I'm going to freeze to death. You can bloody freeze to death.

She gets snow in his face. Runs.

> I haven't my shoes on. Hey!

He catches her. Holds her. There's a gentleness in his touch.

CUT TO:

INT. THE LANDING. MORNING

Elspeth's watching through the telescope.

                    ELSPETH
    Be kissing next.

    CUT TO:

EXT. ELSPETH'S POV/THE SHORE. MORNING

Alex holding Nita. She waits for something to happen. He lets her go.

                    ELSPETH
                    (*voice-over*)
    Missed her chance.

    CUT TO:

INT. THE LANDING. MORNING

Elspeth leaves the telescope and goes down the stairs.

                    ELSPETH
    I'd have had him kissing. He'd have kissed me all right.

    CUT TO:

EXT. THE BEACH RIVER. THE TUNNEL BEACH. MORNING

*Tom's foot slips. He nearly falls. Sam's hand goes out, steadies Tom.
Tom shakes him off.*

                    TOM
    Fuck off.

                    SAM
    Suit yourself.

They're crossing the frozen river. Jumping from stone to stone.

Tom looks out at the ice on the sea.

                    TOM
    Think it goes on for ever?

                    SAM
    It's got to end somewhere.

Tom's staring out.

TOM

What if it doesn't?

SAM

What if?

Tom shrugs.

Sam leaves him. Follows the frozen stream up to its source at the tunnel.

CUT TO:

EXT. THE TOWN BEACH/PROM. MORNING

Alex climbs over the prom rail. Pushes the bike.

ALEX

My feet are dropping off.

Nita walks along with him.

NITA

Go home and get a dry pair of socks, for God's sake.

ALEX

My grandmother's in there. My mother's had her hair cut.
That's a bloody battlefield.

CUT TO:

INT. THE STAIRS. MORNING

Frances running down the stairs. She sees her mother sitting on the sofa.

INT. THE FRONT ROOM. MORNING

Elspeth's staring at her hands. They're shaking. She tries to steady them and can't.

INT. THE STAIRS. MORNING

Frances watches her mother clasp her hands together. Elspeth can't stop the shaking. There's fear in her face.

59

Frances charges into the front room. She thrusts the photographs at her mother.

ELSPETH

What are these? What are they?

FRANCES

Have a look.

ELSPETH

Did you take these?

FRANCES

For a school prospectus.

ELSPETH

A commission?

FRANCES

What's wrong with that?

ELSPETH

Bread and butter.

FRANCES

We have to eat.

ELSPETH

You used to have a light in your eyes.

FRANCES

You're not even looking at them.

ELSPETH

What did you take them with?

FRANCES

The big camera.

ELSPETH

The one I bought you.

FRANCES

Yes. Yes. Thank you for that.

ELSPETH

Make it sound like a curse. Why is it so hard?

FRANCES

What?

ELSPETH

Is saying thank you so hard?

FRANCES

Without the camera you bought me I couldn't have taken this job.

ELSPETH

I thought you'd take people. That's what I thought you wanted it for: people. That's why I bought it.

FRANCES

What's wrong with them?

ELSPETH

Have you nothing exciting to show me?

CUT TO:

EXT. THE TERMINUS. MORNING

Lily rapping on the door of the bus. The bus driver taps his watch.

LILY

We could die of frostbite.

Chloe can't catch her breath.

CHLOE

If I waved a five-pound note he'd open it up.

LILY

If you waved a . . .

CHLOE

What?

LILY

If you had a five-pound note to wave around we'd be taking a taxi. We'd be on Gran Canaria for the winter sunshine if you had a five-pound note and nothing else to do with it but wave it at bus drivers.

She raps hard at the door. It opens under her fist.

Not before time.

She helps Chloe up the bus steps.

CUT TO:

INT. FRONT ROOM. MORNING

Frances looks through the window. A child's pushing at the old chained roundabout. Pushing and pulling. But it only moves to the length of the chain.

> FRANCES
>
> You don't have to keep checking up on me.

> ELSPETH
>
> Do I not?

> FRANCES
>
> I'm all right.

> ELSPETH
>
> Look at you.

> FRANCES
>
> I don't need you.

> ELSPETH
>
> Don't you ever say that to me. I was a young woman when I had you, with a young woman's preoccupations. You taught me to care, my God. Demanded that I . . . that I care. With your screaming and your crying and your wee hands that beat at me and grabbed at me.

Her own hands are gesturing. Out of control. A black-out threatens. She fights it. Frances can only watch.

> You taught me to look after you twenty-four hours of the day. Step by step by step. You cut me out of my old life and then you kept me from it. Step by step the two of us went. So what do you expect?

Frances takes her mother's hands. Holds on to them.

Just because you're all grown up. I've to stop? All that caring.
I've to stop? To know you're all right.

                    FRANCES
I'm fine.

                    ELSPETH
You don't look fine.

                    FRANCES
I'm not sick.

                    ELSPETH
I want the best for you.

The hands escape.

That's all I want. All I've ever wanted. Frances. Cherub.

Frances pushes the photographs at her.

                    FRANCES
I like these. Look. These.

                    ELSPETH
Better you have it now. Better you get it now than the tax
man when I die.

                    FRANCES
I'll pay you back.

                    ELSPETH
Better you have it now than when I'm in my box.

                    FRANCES
That's the school. See. See.

                    ELSPETH
I hated school. My work years, they were the best years. I'd
be working yet.

                    FRANCES
I love this one.

                    ELSPETH
Do you?

FRANCES

Look at the movement in it.

ELSPETH

If you want movement, Frances, make a film.

FRANCES

They're not the final prints. Look. Look at this paper. I'm
trying out different papers. Look at this, Mother. The depth
you get in this.

ELSPETH

Snaps for a school prospectus they'll never hang in the Tate.

FRANCES

This is old this paper. Camera shop man he gave it to me.

ELSPETH

What age is he?

FRANCES

I couldn't afford to buy it.

ELSPETH

Is he married?

FRANCES

Depth you get on it.

ELSPETH

He must like you to give you all that.

FRANCES

I'm not looking for a husband.

ELSPETH

You can't live alone.

FRANCES

I've Alex.

ELSPETH

You're still a young . . . Cutting your hair.

FRANCES

See this.

64

It's damn lonely living on your own. I know that. I like a
colour picture.

                        FRANCES
Here. Here.

                        ELSPETH
Why do you not use colour? The world's in colour, cherub.

CUT TO:

EXT. THE COAST ROAD/THE BUS. MORNING

*The sky's clear blue. The maroon and white bus winds up the coast
road. The snow crunches under its tyres. The hill's sheer above it. The
cliffs below fall away to the frozen sea.*

Lily looks out of the window.

                        LILY
                    (*voice-over*)
Guess what I'm thinking of.

CUT TO:

INT. THE BUS. MORNING

                        CHLOE
The workings of your mind are a mystery to me, Lily.

                        LILY
I'm thinking of a French cake. Pink icing. Will we have a
French cake in the town? Today. After? It's a cremation, after
all. We'll need a treat.

                        CHLOE
I've seen many a nice cremation.

                        LILY
It's not as final, Chloe. You know where you are with a
burial. Permanent, a burial. There's nothing like watching a
coffin slip down into the earth. And the soil thudding down
on the wood. That's a rare treat these days. Factory death we

65

get these days. All this conservation. All this ecology. You'd
think they'd want to save on the gas. Will we have a French
cake Chloe?

Chloe stares at her.

                              CHLOE
Why do you always take the window seat?

CUT TO:

INT. THE FRONT ROOM. MORNING

Elspeth shuffling through the bundle of photographs.

                              ELSPETH
Congratulations.

                              FRANCES
Thank you.

                              ELSPETH
A man could have taken these. There. Does that please you?

                              FRANCES
I'm not quite sure.

                              ELSPETH
Your hair and your work. You're all of a piece now.

Frances decides not to give her mother the pleasure of a reply.

CUT TO:

EXT. MENZIES. MORNING

*Nita and Alex are leaning against the window above an air vent in the
pavement, trying to get a bit of heat. Alex has a pie.*

                              NITA
See mince?

                              ALEX
Don't start.

NITA

Could be eyeballs, for all you know. Could be entrails.

He bites the pie. The ground beef is a pallid grey.

Bum holes, even.

His chewing becomes less enthusiastic.

CUT TO:

INT. THE FRONT ROOM/THE HALL. MORNING

Frances leaving the front room. Collects her boots.

Elspeth follows.

ELSPETH

A happy woman doesn't mutilate herself. I'm not talking about the husband that you lost. A woman that's happy in her work. A happy woman doesn't ruin her own beauty.

Her looks sweeps Frances from top to toe.

FRANCES

This is my body and I can do what I like with it. I can get fat if I like. I can cut my own hair. I happen to think I look good.

ELSPETH

I've seen you look better.

FRANCES

Come on.

ELSPETH

I've seen better photographs.

FRANCES

I'm paid to take them.

The photographs on the mantelpiece blur in and out of focus.

ELSPETH

These are better photographs. Every last one of them. You photographed a death and it dried you up.

FRANCES

Will we go shopping, will we? Your shopping, Mother.

ELSPETH

Show me one picture. One picture that you wanted to take.

Frances sorts through the bundle.

FRANCES

Here.

ELSPETH

That's Alex.

FRANCES

I don't expect you to like it.

ELSPETH

I can see your hand in this. That's Australia.

FRANCES

You like it?

ELSPETH
Maybe he'll have a chance now.

FRANCES
What are you talking about?

ELSPETH
Don't you play the innocent.

FRANCES
You're trespassing, Mother.

ELSPETH
I'm scared to death.

FRANCES
I'm warning you.

ELSPETH
You had no room for that boy in your lives. Don't you walk
away from me. As well he's dead. There. I'll say what has to be
said. You were obsessed the two of you. You're obsessed yet.

She takes a picture from the mantelpiece.

FRANCES
Give it to me.

Elspeth holds on to it.

Give it to me.

*Frances takes the picture. The photograph sucks her in. Jamie at a
window in the rain.*

ELSPETH
Days passing in a dream. And then you'll look. Years will
have passed from out of your grasp. And you'll wonder where
they've gone to. One life that's all. You'll not get the lost
years back.

FRANCES
It was dark blue that raincoat.

She touches the coat. Her wedding ring's loose on her finger.

Elspeth taps the photograph of Alex.

ELSPETH

Here. Here.

FRANCES

The Barrier Reef.

ELSPETH

D'you want to go back there?

FRANCES

Where's your stick?

ELSPETH

I can walk without a stick. Do you want to go back to
Australia?

FRANCES

Where is it?

ELSPETH

I didn't bring it. You're not answering me. You liked
Australia, didn't you?

FRANCES

Did you walk along here without a stick?

ELSPETH

I did.

FRANCES

In the snow?

ELSPETH

They didn't clear a path in front of me.

FRANCES

You're a fool, Mother.

ELSPETH

I thought I did rather well.

FRANCES

You could have killed yourself.

ELSPETH

I can do without a stick. I'm getting better.

Frances takes an umbrella from the corner by the front door.

FRANCES

Use this.

ELSPETH

You can keep it.

FRANCES

Mother.

ELSPETH

I'm not using that. I don't like it.

FRANCES

What's wrong with it?

ELSPETH

There's a lot of things I don't like that you have.

Frances leaves her mother and goes into the kitchen.

That you do. I keep quiet about it.

FRANCES

When are you ever quiet?

CUT TO:

EXT. THE TUNNEL. MORNING

Sam howling down the tunnel. The noise reverberates.

TOM

What do you do for an encore?

Sam does a perfect owl hoot. It's eerie in the tunnel under the prom with the dark, frozen river running through it.

SAM

Good, eh?

TOM

What's that noise?

What?

There's an indefinable something in the tunnel. The boys stay where they are. The silence is unbearable. Tom's nerve breaks. He runs. Sam follows.

CUT TO:

INT. KITCHEN. MORNING

Elspeth shouts through to the kitchen.

ELSPETH
Was it sex you and yon dead man? Was that what it was?

Frances takes a carton of orange juice out of the fridge.

Elspeth comes through to the kitchen and shuts the fridge door.

I don't want you to take me to do my shopping.

Frances drinks the juice straight from the carton.

Elspeth puts a glass down for her. Frances ignores it.

I don't need you.

FRANCES
I'm to sit at home, am I? And wait for Casualty to call.

Elspeth starts wiping surfaces with a cloth. It knocks the breath out of her to do it.

ELSPETH
I'm getting better.

FRANCES
It's all right for you to tell me what to do. That's all right is it?

ELSPETH
Why do you hate me?

FRANCES
Jesus.

She bangs the empty carton down on top of the fridge. Her mother picks it up and puts it in the bin.

ELSPETH

You always loved your father best.

FRANCES

Please.

ELSPETH

Don't you think I didn't know. Girls and their fathers.

FRANCES

Where's the tears, Mother?

ELSPETH

Are you going back to Australia?

Frances grabs a bowl of olives from the fridge and eats them.

FRANCES

No tears?

ELSPETH

I need a drink to cry. A half bottle of Gordon's then I'll cry. I'll cry all right. Gin tears. The only sort I've got left. My tear ducts have dried up. It's only the gin that can make me lachrymose.

Frances sits on the arm of the kitchen chair laughing.

D'you call that breakfast?

Frances offers her an olive. She doesn't take one.

Let me try without the stick, Frances. I hate the stick. If I fall you're there.

FRANCES

Not always.

ELSPETH

I don't like shops. I don't like shopping.

FRANCES

You have to eat tomorrow.

ELSPETH

Bugger tomorrow, Frances. I'm not talking about tomorrow.
You're with me today and we could have fun. No stick,
Frances. Just this day. No umbrella. I like a bright umbrella.
Vivid colours. I must have brightness in my life. Look at your
hair.

FRANCES

It's growing.

ELSPETH

Not fast enough. Did you like Australia?

FRANCES

Yes.

ELSPETH

And Alex?

FRANCES

He'd live there if he could.

ELSPETH

Look at the day it is. Bugger the shops. Take your camera and
we'll go out. Take your camera. And I'll be with you. I'll be
quiet, Frances. Take me out to work with you. I'd like to
watch you work.

FRANCES

It's freezing out there.

ELSPETH

I can put a jumper on. I've my fur coat. You've a jumper you
can lend me. Please, Frances. Please.

Frances is caught somewhere between a smile and a sigh.

CUT TO:

EXT. THE TUNNEL BEACH. MORNING

*Sam and Tom tromping along the beach. They go round the headland
into a landscape of ice and snow and grey volcanic rock.*

74

Think there's something in there?

TOM

Naaa.

SAM

Think there is, though?

TOM

Any cigs?

SAM

No.

TOM

Neither me.

He hugs himself against the cold. Turns his back to the wind.

I've a Mars bar.

SAM

Wanker.

Sam flicks at seaweed with a stick.

TOM

Want a bit? Half and half.

Sam shrugs.

TOM

King-size Mars bar.

SAM

Half and half?

TOM

Uh huh.

SAM

Gonnie measure it?

TOM

Got a ruler?

SAM

Uh huh.

Tom takes out a book, lays it flat on the rock. Sam has the ruler out.

TOM

Give us it.

He measures the Mars bar. Fifteen centimetres.

SAM

Seven and a half. Mark it.

TOM

Got a knife?

SAM

I'll cut it.

TOM

My Mars bar.

SAM

My knife.

Sam brings out his Swiss army knife.

TOM

Bloody hell. Crockett sees that he'll do you.

SAM

Crockett's not gonnie see it.

TOM

Threw Shanks out for carrying a knife.

SAM

Wanker Shanks was. I'm not gonnie use the fucking thing.
Crockett's a wanker. Gonnie tell him?

TOM

I cut the Mars bar.

SAM

Crockett's a pouf.

76

Sam throws Tom the knife.

    Seven and a half, mind.

Tom opens the knife.

TOM

    Good knife.

Tom cuts the Mars bar. Throws the knife to Sam. Holds out half the Mars bar.

SAM

    Chuck it, then.

TOM

    Closer we sit together, warmer we'll be.

SAM

    You a pouf?

TOM

    D'you want this?

SAM

    Wanker.

But he comes in close. They sit on their bags, the pair of them, in the shelter of the rocks. Tear back the paper. Munch on the bar. Side by side. The sound of laughter.

CUT TO:

INT. HALL. MORNING

Elspeth laughing. A rain of jumpers showers down on her.

Frances is pulling them out of the seaman's chest.

ELSPETH

    My God, Frances. The colours in this. This is the one I'll have.

Elspeth slips it on. The jumpers keep on flying.

Comes down to my knees, Frances. Stop. Stop.

Elspeth's at the mirror.

What do I look like?

FRANCES
Fine.

ELSPETH
Is that my face?

FRANCES
You look great.

ELSPETH
You should change on the inside, do you know that? That would be fairer. I get a fright when I look in the mirror. I'm the same inside as I was at seventeen. And look at me. Look at me. I hate my old face.

Frances picks up Elspeth's coat.

Give me a sensible jumper in keeping with my years.

FRANCES
Suits you.

She holds her mother's coat out for her. Shrugs her into it. Rubs the collar against her mother's face. The fur tickles.

Elspeth laughs.

ELSPETH
More. More.

Frances holds the fur to her mother's cheek. Strokes her mother's skin with the backs of her fingers.

CUT TO:

EXT. THE ROCKS. MORNING

Tom licks an ooze of caramel off the wrapper.

CUT TO:

INT. THE HALL. MORNING

Frances puts on her coat. She shoves her fingers through her hair. Dares her mother to comment.

Elspeth refrains. She picks up a Nikon camera from the table. Offers it to Frances.

> ELSPETH
> Here.

Frances hesitates but she takes the camera. Elspeth sweeps past her.

> CUT TO:

EXT. THE BEACH. DAY

Tom runs his tongue all over the wrapper to pick up any stray scrap of chocolate.

> CUT TO:

INT./EXT. THE PORCH/THE BACK DOOR. MORNING

Frances at the open back door. The sun flares up from the snow in the yard.

> FRANCES
> Shouldn't wear fur.

Elspeth crosses the yard.

> ELSPETH
> Died long ago, Frances.

She has to tug at the wooden gate to open it. The effort takes her breath away.

> Long, long, long ago.

She grabs on to the railings.

> Forty years I've had this coat. Waste if I didn't wear it.

She eases herself along the passage.

> CUT TO:

79

EXT. MENZIES. MORNING

Nita's watching Alex. He screws up the pie bag and throws it in a bin.

ALEX

Come here.

NITA

What for?

CUT TO:

EXT. THE FRONT GATE. MORNING

Elspeth pauses for a moment, hanging on to the rail. Catches her breath. The ice and snow stretch away from her. The long wharf. The wind blows across the old harbour.

FRANCES

Take my arm.

ELSPETH

I'll do no such thing.

She goes out the gate.

Frances could insist on helping. She makes herself watch instead. Her mother walks briskly across the old harbour past the roundabout.

CUT TO:

EXT. MENZIES/BRUCE'S WYND. MORNING

ALEX

Shit.

Alex catches sight of Elspeth and Frances coming down the side of the old harbour. He grabs his bike, yanks Nita to her feet, pulls her along the road and into Bruce's Wynd. Hides in the shadows.

NITA

What the hell?

ALEX

Quiet!

Nita sneaks a look round the corner of the lane.

NITA

Is that your mum?

The sun gleams out.

Elspeth and Frances are coming along the street.

ALEX

What's she doing?

NITA

Nothing. Talking.

ALEX

Sniping, more like. Which way are they going?

NITA

How do I know?

Alex sneaks a look, watches them go.

ALEX

Lighthouse. They'll be a while.

He turns to her. They're quite close in the shadows.

You're soaking.

There's a wisp of hair caught at the corner of Nita's mouth. He carefully tucks it behind her ear.

NITA

How's your feet?

ALEX

What feet?

Alex checks that Frances is out of sight.

ALEX

The house is empty.

Nita just looks at him.

Come home with me?

Nita goes on looking.

NITA

If you like.

Alex walks out of Bruce's Wynd, collects his bike from outside Menzies, walks towards the old harbour. Nita stays where she is. He doesn't look back. She sticks her hands in her jacket pocket. Head down, not looking at him, she follows.

CUT TO:

EXT. THE ROCK BEACH. MORNING

Sam leans back, puts his hand behind him. Leaps to his feet, screaming.

TOM

What the fuck's up with you?

SAM

It's a worm! It's a worm!

TOM

It's not.

SAM

It's a big fat skooshy worm.

TOM

You scared of worms?

SAM

No.

TOM

Ay you are.

SAM

Ay I'm not.

TOM

Scared of a wee worm.

SAM

Look at it. It's a squelcher.

Tom lifts up a stick. Waves it at Sam.

TOM

It's a condom.

The condom droops down from the end of the stick.

SAM

Shit.

TOM

It's been used.

SAM

I touched that. I fucking touched that.

TOM

Found one up a tree once. Six metres up.

SAM

I've geek on my fingers. I'm gonnie die.

TOM

'Magine doing it up a tree. 'Magine doin' it.

SAM

Help me, God. Help me, Jesus.

TOM

You prayin'?

SAM

What if?

TOM

You prayin' to God.

SAM

I'm prayin' to my Aunt Fanny. What d'you think I'm doin'?

TOM

Probably didn't do it up a tree. Probably threw it there after. What do you do with them after? Eh? They don't tell you that in them sex education films. Call that education? Never make it look like anything you might want to have a go at. If it's like that, doing it, like them people in the films, I'm going to be a wanker. I'll be a wanker all my life. It's the only fucking option. If my balls drop. If they ever drop. My balls are never gonnie drop. Ron's balls have dropped to his knees. They've lived a life his balls and mine haven't even entered the arena yet. I've got this empty bag of skin between my legs that sticks to my thighs when I get hot. Waiting, just waiting. Every morning I wake up, I leap out of the bed. Down go the boxers. I look. Empty. Dear God help me. Christ Jesus lend us a hand.

Sam's washing his hands in the snow.

Sewage runs down this beach.

You're washing your hands in shit.

Sam looks at his hands. A small bleat escapes him. He wipes his hands down the sides of his blazer.

Tom's drawn by the frozen sea. The wind blows. The sun shines on the ice. The glitter pulls him. He almost walks out on it.

CUT TO:

84

EXT. THE CLIFF WALK. DAY

*Frances and Elspeth walk along the path at the cliff edge; the drop is
sheer. Elspeth should be on Frances's arm, but she isn't. Her
determination to hold on to her independence is fearsome.*

CUT TO:

EXT. THE ROCK BEACH. DAY

*Sam, kicking at sticks and seaweed, calls to Tom who's still mesmerized
by the world he sees out on the ice.*

SAM

Could light a fire.

TOM

You got matches?

SAM

Some.

TOM

Nothing to burn.

85

SAM

Dry seaweed. Sticks. Rubbish. Plenty about.

TOM

I'd like a fire.

CUT TO:

EXT. THE CLIFF WALK. DAY

Elspeth walks ahead of Frances. She has to stop because the way's steep. She pretends she's looking at the view. Frances catches up. Elspeth walks on. They're heading for the sandwich kiosk near the beach.

CUT TO:

INT. THE HALL. FRANCES'S HOUSE. DAY

Nita's wet and shivering. She comes down the steps into the hall. Watching Alex from behind her hair. Waiting for him to say something . . . anything. But he doesn't.

NITA

Colder in here than it was outside.

ALEX

Heating's bust.

NITA

Can't you get it fixed?

ALEX

Been bust for ages. Want me to warm you up?

She turns away from him. The house is spacious. It has a certain beauty.

Nita touches a photograph. It shifts slightly.

Alex comes up behind her softly, on stockinged soles. He puts the photograph back exactly where it was.

NITA

Sorry.

86

ALEX

D'you want a bath?

INT. THE STAIRS. DAY

Alex heads up the stairs.

NITA

What d'you mean?

She follows.

ALEX

Hot bath. That'll warm you.

NITA

If you don't mind.

Past all the photographs.

These your dad?

ALEX

The rest of her pictures are in the studio. Some in the darkroom. Studio's a mess.

INT. THE MIDDLE LANDING. DAY

Alex holds open the bathroom door. Nita goes inside. Stands looking at him.

ALEX

There's a lock.

NITA

Don't forget your feet.

Alex wriggles his toes.

Nita laughs. Alex smiles.

Well.

She shuts the door, peeping round it as she does. The door clicks.

Alex dives into his bedroom.

INT. ALEX'S BEDROOM. DAY

Alex grabs a sweatshirt from the bottom of the wardrobe. Wheeches off shirt, tie and sweater all in one go. Scrambles into the sweatshirt.

CUT TO:

EXT. THE ROCK BEACH. DAY

Tom throwing down an armful of the stuff he's collected.

TOM
Give us the matches, then. Come on.

SAM
Won't burn like that.

TOM
It'll burn.

SAM
There's an art to a beach fire.

Sam's putting stones round in a ring.

TOM
You know, do you?

SAM
Uh huh.

TOM
You would.

Sam builds a fire on the stones.

Could do with a cig.

Sam lights a match. Some of the fire catches.

DISSOLVE:

INT. THE HALL. DAY

Alex has a fire going in the grate. He uses brass bellows. Yellow flames lick up the chimney.

DISSOLVE:

EXT. THE ROCK BEACH. DAY

The fire's crackling. There's a glow on Sam's face. The black ice on the rocks reflects the flames.

> SAM

Hey!

Tom's peeing. The stream of hot pee melts the ice. The reflection dies.

You could help.

> TOM

'M busy.

Tom's examining his penis. Sam looks over Tom's shoulder.

> SAM

What do you call that?

> TOM

Maggot.

> SAM

Know what you should do?

> TOM

What?

> SAM

Rub some Deep Heat on.

> TOM

What for?

> SAM

Make it grow.

> TOM

How?

> SAM

Heat.

> TOM

Eh?

SAM

They swell in the heat.

TOM

Do they?

SAM

Swell in the heat. Shrivel in the cold. Deep Heat makes them grow. Penetrates.

TOM

Have you got any?

SAM

What?

TOM

Deep Heat.

SAM

Yup.

TOM

Where?

SAM

In my bag.

TOM

Why?

SAM

Got it off my brother.

TOM

Eh?

SAM

He uses it.

TOM

On his dong?

SAM

Fucking huge one he's got.

                    TOM
Uses Deep Heat?

                    SAM
Probably does.

He digs out the Deep Heat. An old tube wrinkled and bent.

                    TOM
You tried it?

                    SAM
Not yet.

                    TOM
Going to?

                    SAM
Only got this much. Want it?

                    TOM
D'you?

                    SAM
You can have it.

Tom takes the top off. Sniffs.

                    TOM
Jesus.

                    SAM
What?

                    TOM
Fucking stench, Sam.

                    SAM
That's the goodness in it.

                    TOM
Brings tears to your eyes.

                    SAM
It's not your eyes you're using it on. Male strippers use it.

TOM

How do you know?

SAM

They need big ones, so they use this. That's all the women
are interested in. No good having a maggot if you're a male
stripper.

TOM

I don't want to be a stripper.

SAM

Never know when it might come in handy. There's no such
thing as security these days. Need to be able to turn your
hand to anything. My dad's a fucking good architect. He's
been made redundant. Sits on the sofa he does. Grey in the
face. He'd work in a pub. He'd do anything. Take his clothes
off if it wouldn't be an obscenity, he's so old. Wrinkled balls
he's got, and a big vein running down his dick. Varicose veins
on his dick, he's got. And piles. Imagine a stripper with piles.
Try it.

Tom squeezes a wriggle of cream on to his finger.

A good dollop.

TOM

That's all there is.

SAM

Better than nothing.

TOM

Will it make my balls drop?

SAM

Dunno.

Tom puts his hand down inside his trousers and rubs the Deep Heat in.

SAM

Put it away. Keep it warm.

Tom holds his trousers closed. Thinks.

TOM

It's burning a bit.

SAM

That's it working.

Tom starts wriggling.

Keep still.

TOM

Sam.

SAM

What?

TOM

It's burning.

SAM

Bound to a bit.

TOM

Sam.

SAM

What?

TOM

Sam.

SAM

For fuck's sake.

TOM

It's burning. It's burning. My penis is on fire.

SAM

Jesus. Keep your keks up.

Sam runs down to the edge of the sea. Grabs some ice.

TOM

Help my Bob. Help my Bob.

SAM

Someone'll see.

TOM

Help me. Help me. Help me.

SAM

Gonnie get yourself arrested.

TOM

My dong's falling off.

Sam runs back up the beach. Drops the ice in Tom's pants.

Tom screams.

SAM

Quiet!

Tom doesn't move. Sam doesn't move. The world's still.

SAM

Better?

TOM

Oh fuck. Oh fuck. Fuck, fuck, fuck. Mammy, Daddy, Mammy, Daddy, fuck, fuck, fuck.

SAM

Is it better? Is it? Is it?

TOM

Mammy, Daddy. Mammy, Daddy.

SAM

Shut up, for fuck's sake.

TOM

Oh shite, oh shite.

SAM

Want me to belt you?

TOM

Bugger, bugger, bugger.

SAM

I'll belt you if you don't shut up.

Tom's persuaded.

It was only a wee bit of cream.

TOM

You try it. You try it. Just you bloody try it.

SAM

You cryin'?

TOM

Bloody cry if I want to.

SAM

Has it grown?

TOM

Fucking dropped off, that's what it's done.

SAM

Has it though?

Tom looks.

TOM

No.

SAM

You look like you've wet yourself.

Tom stands close to the fire.

Wasn't my fault.

Tom doesn't speak.

Could've worked.

Sam digs around in his bag.

Here.

He's holding a cigarette out to Tom.

TOM

'S'at for me?

Sam shrugs, goes to take it away.

Give it.

Sam passes it over.

Want half?

SAM

Naaaa.

TOM

Got a match?

SAM

Your face an' a pile of shite.

TOM

Fuck off.

Sam strikes a match.

Tom bends to the match cupped in Sam's hands. Takes a long haul on the cigarette.

Jeeeees . . . us. This is good Sam. This is a good bit. Got to know the good bits.

CUT TO:

EXT. THE KIOSK/THE KIOSK BEACH. DAY

The lighthouse is garishly cheerful, very white against the blue sky.

KIOSK LADY

Two teas?

ELSPETH

Don't put milk in mine.

She's shouting back to Frances, waiting for sandwiches at the kiosk.

FRANCES

One black.

ELSPETH

Turnips – they feed the cows on.

Elspeth's walking much too quickly down the slipway to the beach.

I'd abolish turnips from the face of this earth. How can there
be a benign God if there's turnips.

Snatches of what she's saying reach Frances.

ELSPETH

I can taste turnips in the milk in my tea in winter. Don't you
put milk in my tea.

Elspeth's on the rocks. She looks desperately unsafe.

Frances is watching her. Calls.

FRANCES

Wait, will you?

KIOSK LADY

Corned beef on brown, do you?

FRANCES

Pardon?

Elspeth's stumbling.

ELSPETH

There'd better not be turnips in Heaven when I get there.

KIOSK LADY

She needs watched.

FRANCES

Is that the ham?

She grabs the sandwiches.

Elspeth puts a hand down, saves herself from falling.

Frances snatches the teas.

Thank you.

CUT TO:

INT. SKINNERS TEA ROOM. DAY

Chloe's peering in from the narrow street outside.

There's a few people in there. A dog lies under one table.

A small boy, with beans and chips in front of him, stares at Chloe's big face, looming at him through the window. He's got a fistful of chips.

> CHLOE
> (*voice-over*)
> Will we go in Lily? Will we?

CUT TO:

EXT. THE BEACH. DAY

Frances running along the beach to join her mother. Balancing sandwiches and tea.

Elspeth's walking faster and faster. There's a bite in her voice.

> ELSPETH
> You think it'll last for ever. That's what you think.

> FRANCES
> Be careful.

She walks parallel to her mother. The camera's over her shoulder. The teas are one on top of the other. The sandwiches are tucked under her arm. Her free hand hovers under Elspeth's elbow.

> ELSPETH
> My year started in September when you were young. Up the hill to Christmas. Roller-coaster ride to spring. I know we fought. Near scratched each other's eyes out. I like a fight.

Elspeth stumbles on a stone. Frances's hand goes out. She grabs her mother's arm. Elspeth shakes her off.

> FRANCES
> Will you slow down?

> ELSPETH
> Don't you speak to me like that.

                    FRANCES
You're going to fall.

                    ELSPETH
I can walk this beach as well as you can.

                    FRANCES
You'll break your ankle.

                    ELSPETH
I'm not an invalid, Frances. I can go for a walk if I like.

                    FRANCES
Come on, we'll have a picnic.

                    ELSPETH
Dear God, if I thought I was an invalid I'd give up here and
now.

She really strides out.

                    FRANCES
What are you trying to prove?

                    ELSPETH
Get your skates on.

                    FRANCES
You're on your own, Mother. I'm not playing.

She stops walking. Watches her mother.

                    ELSPETH
I'm not ready to face the flames.

A stone turns. Elspeth falls.

                    FRANCES
Jesus, Mother.

*Elspeth stays still. Frances runs towards her. The tea spills over her
hand. She drops it. Sucks at her burnt hand as she runs.*

CUT TO:

INT. THE HALL. FRANCES'S HOUSE. DAY

Alex sitting by the roaring fire.

> NITA
> (*off*)

Alex!

Alex turns his head.

CUT TO:

INT. THE BATHROOM. DAY

The bathroom's aglow with the colours from the stained-glass window.
Nita's in the bath. She pushes her hair back from her face.
The towel rail's empty.

> NITA

There's no towels.

CUT TO:

INT. THE HALL. DAY

Alex stares.

> NITA
> (*off*)

Alex?

Alex gets to his feet. Gallops up the stairs.

CUT TO:

EXT. THE KIOSK. BEACH. DAY

Frances reaches her mother.

> FRANCES
> (*yelling*)

You're an old fool, do you know that? Get up. Look at you.
Take a stick? No, no not you. Is this your second childhood,
Mother? Jesus Christ, I'm glad I wasn't around for the first. I

hope you're hurt. Do you hear me? I hope you're in agony.
Are you listening to me? You deserve all you get. Get up. Get
up now.

*Silence descends. Elspeth's like a child lying there. Frances kneels down
beside her.*

                         FRANCES
Mother?

                         ELSPETH
Take that look off your face. I'm not dead yet.

CUT TO:

INT. THE BATHROOM DOOR. DAY

*Alex takes towels from the camphor wood chest. He taps on the
bathroom door. His hands tighten on the towels.*

*Nita's head and a bare arm poke round the door. Alex pushes the
bundle at her.*

                         ALEX
Give me your clothes.

                         NITA
What?

                         ALEX
You want me to dry them, don't you?

*As she turns to get them, he glimpses the long white line of her body
through the gap in the door.*

She shoves the clothes at him, gripping the towels to her.

The door closes on Alex. To his regret.

CUT TO:

EXT. THE KIOSK BEACH. DAY

Elspeth heaves herself into a sitting position. Frances tries to help.

                         ELSPETH
I'll do it my own way.

Frances stands back.

Look at that.

Elspeth has a cut on her knee.

The ruination of a good pair of tights.

Frances dabs at her mother's knee with a napkin from the kiosk.

It won't kill me.

She takes the napkin and tends to her own knee.

                         FRANCES
Are you getting up at any point?

                         ELSPETH
I quite like it down here.

Elspeth bum shuffles on to a rock. She isn't capable of getting up.

                         FRANCES
Let me take you home.

                         ELSPETH
I'm all right, Frances. I'm all right. I'm all right.

Her hand's beating on the rock.

CUT TO:

INT. SKINNERS. DAY

*Lily and Chloe are sitting at a window table. Lily pushes away a plate
of watery, uneaten scrambled egg.*

                         LILY
Manning's Funeral Parlour is off my list. You'll not use
Manning's when I die.

                         CHLOE
I'll make a note of that.

LILY

If you set out to go to a funeral in the morning, a funeral in the morning is what you expect to get.

CHLOE

After all, it's old.

LILY

Eh?

CHLOE

The hearse, Lily.

LILY

You're old. I'm old. We got here without breaking down.

CHLOE

You can't have a funeral without the body.

LILY

I'm not disputing that. They should have checked their hearse. That's all I'm saying.

CHLOE

Delayed till three o'clock, Lily. It's not as if it's cancelled.

Lily takes her glasses off and peers at the cake trolley.

The boy's mother fastens him into a coat. He stares at Chloe.

LILY

Millefeuille.

CHLOE

Will we share it, Lily? Will we?

She sees the boy staring at her. She stares right back. Neither of them smiles. His mother takes him out of Skinners. His head's still turning, staring.

CUT TO:

EXT. THE KIOSK BEACH. DAY

Frances sits beside Elspeth.

FRANCES

Corned beef or ham?

ELSPETH

Has the ham brown sauce?

FRANCES

Mustard.

ELSPETH

I like brown sauce.

FRANCES

Take the corned beef.

Elspeth doesn't.

Take it, Mother.

Elspeth takes the sandwich. Puts it down on the rock.

ELSPETH

I eat when I'm hungry. I drink when I'm dry.

Frances bites into her sandwich.

ELSPETH

I'd have liked a cup of tea.

Frances does not reply.

The world glitters around them.

DISSOLVE:

EXT. SAM'S FIRE. DAY

Sam's fire flares. He chucks more paper on to it. Stares into the flames.

DISSOLVE:

INT. SKINNERS. DAY

Chloe's fork flashes in the sunlight. The millefeuille*'s on a plate in front of her.*

CHLOE

Go on.

Lily takes a dainty corner. Chloe watches her eat it. Smiles at the pleasure in Lily's face. Takes a piece herself.

The cafe's very silent. The sun shines through the window.

SAM
(*voice-over*)
As a white candle in a holy place
So is the beauty of an aged face.

Lily and Chloe eat in the sunlight. A whisper of an image of Elspeth.

DISSOLVE:

EXT. THE LIGHTHOUSE ROCK. DAY

Elspeth sits in the sunlight. Frances watches her. Elspeth's face is calm. She's not fighting. Her weariness shows.

SAM
(*voice-over*)
As the spent radiance of the winter sun
So is a woman with her travail done.

DISSOLVE:

EXT. SAM'S FIRE. DAY

Sam's singing in the sunlight. A pure clear boy's voice. Tom's riveted.

SAM

Her brood gone from her
And her thoughts as still,
As the water
Under a ruined mill.

TOM
Jesus. Where'd you get that?

SAM
Choir.

                              TOM
     Bit fucking sad, isn't it?

                              SAM
     I like it.

                              TOM
     Have them rolling in the aisles, that. How many things do you
     go to?

                              SAM
     Choir. Scouts.

Silence.

     What? What?

                              TOM
     Shit! Fire's going down.

Sam leaps to his feet.

     What're you jumping up for?

                              SAM
     Need more stuff.

Sam's off collecting.

                              TOM
     Never at peace.

                              SAM
     Don't sit still too long. You'll freeze to death.

He's heading back round the headland.

     CUT TO:

EXT. THE KIOSK BEACH. DAY

Frances watches Elspeth light a cigarette.

                              ELSPETH
     What're you looking at?

FRANCES

I can look.

ELSPETH

Not at me. Not like that you can't.

FRANCES

You shouldn't smoke.

ELSPETH

I'll do what I like. If I can't do that now, when can I do it?

She pulls Frances's clothes to rights.

I always had you nice when you were wee. My own clothes cost me nothing.

Her voice becomes vague. Her hands gesture. Plucks at her clothes, her hair. The hands grasp at consciousness.

I'd get up. I'd queue in the sales for my clothes. Wee suits. Wee box jackets. Wee grey suits? You? You never had a sale garment on your back.

Frances catches hold of her hands.

FRANCES

Don't.

ELSPETH

What? What is it for God's sake?

FRANCES

Don't wave your hands about.

ELSPETH

I'm not. I'm not, Frances. I don't know what's wrong with you. Cherub?

FRANCES

Don't.

She lets go of her mother's hands. Walks away to the sea's edge.

The sound of a fire sparking.

CUT TO:

INT. THE HALL. FRANCES'S HOUSE. DAY

The pictures of Frances's husband stacked around the fireplace glow in the firelight. Alex sits facing them, staring into the fire.

CUT TO:

EXT. THE ROCK BEACH. DAY

Tom sitting at Sam's bright fire.

CUT TO:

INT. THE HALL. DAY

Alex turns Nita's sweatshirt. It's on the fire guard steaming in the heat from the flames. The bathroom door clicks. He turns.

CUT TO:

INT. THE MIDDLE LANDING. DAY

Nita slips out of the bathroom wrapped in a towel. Glances in the open bedroom doors. Trails her hand along the banister. Heads for the stairs up to the studio.

CUT TO:

EXT. SAM'S FIRE. DAY

Tom picks up a dog-end. Smooths it out.

CUT TO:

INT. THE STUDIO. DAY

Nita pushes open the door.

There are mirrors in the studio, wooden chests, lights on stands, cameras on tripods. The floor's stripped and scratched. Pieces of velvet hang here and there. It's a dishevelled work-place but it's obvious that it was once loved. Some canvases are stacked in a corner. One stands on an easel covered with a soft grey square of silk.

Nita pulls the scarf off, drapes it round herself. The painting's exposed.

*A landscape with a red glow at its heart. Thick textured paint. Nita
runs her fingertips over it. There's velvet on a chest. She lets the silk
fall. Takes off the towel. Picks up the velvet. Drapes it round herself.
Turns round and round in the mirror. The room shines with light.*

CUT TO:

EXT. SAM'S FIRE. DAY

*Tom holding an ember up to the dog-end. The ice beyond the fire
glitters. Tom's mesmerized by it.*

CUT TO:

EXT. THE KIOSK BEACH. DAY

Elspeth gets herself up from the rock. Calls to Frances.

ELSPETH
It's good this what we're doing today. Is this not good?

FRANCES
Yes.

ELSPETH
Are you enjoying yourself? Are you?

FRANCES
Yes, Mother. Yes, I am.

Elspeth joins Frances at the sea's edge.

ELSPETH
I'd not have had you hurt. You'd have better borne it if I'd died.

FRANCES
Please, Mother.

ELSPETH
Don't you think I'd have taken his place. I prayed God to take
me in his stead.

FRANCES
You were safe enough offering. Doesn't work like that, does
it? Does it?

109

ELSPETH

My coat's warm. Deep pockets on this coat. I'm in love with my coat, Frances. Feel the air, cherub. Know where the good bits are. Seize them, Frances. Grab and hold hard. Hold very hard.

There's a desperate vitality in Elspeth. Frances can't bear it. She has to walk away.

CUT TO:

INT. THE STUDIO. DAY

Nita sees Alex's reflection in the mirror watching her.

NITA

Do you think I look like a boy?

ALEX

You look nice.

NITA

I don't look like a girl, though.

She looks beautiful in the velvet.

ALEX

Eh?

NITA

If you cut off my head and stuck it on a pole, it'd be a boy's head. Anybody looking at it. Standing there. That's a boy's head they'd say. Poor chap. I've got boy's knees.

Look.

Exposes one knee.

Knobbles.

She bangs at her knee with her fist.

ALEX

Don't do that.

Feel this.

Flexes her bicep.

Come on, have a feel of this.

He does.

Well?

ALEX

Very nice.

NITA

Strong?

ALEX

Very strong.

His fingers linger on her arm.

Take off the fancy dress.

He's trespassed. She walks away down the stairs, trailing velvet as she goes, leaving Alex alone in the light-filled studio.

CUT TO:

EXT. THE WIDE BEACH. DAY

The sun flares down on to Frances, ahead of Elspeth walking along the shore.

Elspeth yells.

ELSPETH

When are you going?

FRANCES

What?

ELSPETH

Are you going? When are you going? Simple question. I'm not a fool, Frances.

Frances walks back to her mother.

III

FRANCES

Give me a cigarette.

ELSPETH

I don't blame you.

FRANCES

Give me one.

She takes a cigarette. Elspeth lights it for her.

FRANCES

Cold?

ELSPETH

It's a good coat this.

FRANCES

Let me know when you want to go back.

Frances walks on.

ELSPETH

Suits me this.

She's hurling this at her daughter.

My God it's bleak. I love it. I like weather. Definite weather.
When it rains I like it pelting down. Stotting off the
pavements, I like it. And the wind. I like a good blow.
Sunshine. Couldn't be doing with it all the time and never a
cloud in the sky. Look at this.

Her look takes in the whole landscape.

Clean it up and there's nowhere on this earth could beat it for
beauty.

CUT TO:

EXT. THE TUNNEL. DAY

Sam steps in a pile of shit.

SAM

Jesus.

He kicks at the loose stones at the mouth of the tunnel to get the shit off his shoes. The tunnel draws him. He sees something. The darkness frightens him but he goes in.

CUT TO:

EXT. THE WIDE BEACH. DAY

Frances puts the camera down on the rock and walks towards the sea.

ELSPETH
You'll miss the seasons when you go. It's the weather gets me up in the morning. There's nothing else I've got to get up for.

FRANCES
I don't know if I'm going. I don't know what I'm doing. I haven't made up my mind, Mother. That's the truth.

Blue cigarette smoke rises.

ELSPETH
You tell me. Go on. What have I got to get up for?

FRANCES
Stop it.

ELSPETH
I get up to fight my body, that's what I get up for. And sometimes I win. For an hour or two I win. A day or two if I'm lucky.

CUT TO:

EXT. THE TUNNEL. DAY

Sam approaching a cardboard box in among the rocks. He's wary. He looks into the box. A look of relief crosses his face.

CUT TO:

EXT. THE WIDE BEACH. DAY

Frances looking at the sea. Looking anywhere but at her mother as:

ELSPETH

Do you think I look to you? Do you? Do you think I need
you? I don't need you. There isn't a living soul that I need. I
look at you and I don't envy you. You make it hard. Living.
You think you're so much better. Dear God. I haven't made
such a mess of it.

Frances puts her hands over her ears, cigarette in hand.

I don't expect anything from you. I've had little enough, God
knows. You could tell me straight. Are you going? Are you
staying? You're a closed person. After . . . after what
happened to you . . . I thought we would draw in. I thought
you might need . . . A person . . . I don't care, Frances. I
don't care who it is. A person needs to be needed. And if you
don't need me, you could . . . you could lie. Frances! If
you're not going to smoke that cigarette why did you take it? I
know you're listening.

Frances's hands are still over her ears.

CUT TO:

EXT. THE FROZEN RIVER. DAY

Sam crossing the river carrying the box. Cradling it. Stepping very carefully to protect it.

CUT TO:

EXT. THE WIDE BEACH. DAY

ELSPETH
Are you going to pick up that camera?

FRANCES
Yes.

ELSPETH
When?

Frances won't answer.

What did we come out here for?

FRANCES
You tell me.

ELSPETH
Why do you not get angry?

Frances looks at her mother.

Not with me. With him. With your husband. Nothing wrong with anger. It's better than Australia. Healthier. I'm angry with your husband. I look at what he's done to you. I'm angry all right. Bugger Australia.

FRANCES
Jamie never went there.

ELSPETH
What?

FRANCES
I could leave him behind me. If I go. When I wake in the morning. That's what I want. That's all I want. To leave him behind.

ELSPETH
Go to Carnoustie.

FRANCES
What?

ELSPETH
If you're leaving your husband and uprooting your son to go
somewhere Jamie never went. I just bet he didn't go to
Carnoustie . . . He'd hate your hair.

*Frances just looks at her mother. Elspeth sees the hurt in her daughter's
eyes. She gets up from the rock. Walks down the beach. Calls back.*

Pick up your camera. Pick it up, Frances.

CUT TO:

EXT. SAM'S FIRE. DAY

Sam putting the box down on a rock.

SAM
Make you forget your troubles, eh?

Tom's fastened on the world beyond the flames. Shivering.

Fucking look will you?

Tom looks in.

TOM
Jesus.

Sam laughs.

Can I touch?

SAM
What you asking me for?

Tom puts his hand into the box. Takes out a kitten.

TOM
Where'd'you find them? Sweetheart. The blue eyes he's got.

116

SAM

She.

Sam takes out the other one.

TOM

How d'you know?

SAM

Boy wouldn't look at you like that.

TOM

Eh?

SAM

Tortoiseshell. Don't get boy ones.

TOM

Look at her then.

He's cradling the kitten.

What they doin' here?

SAM

Left them to die.

TOM

What kinda bastard'd it take to kill a wee thing like this?

The kitten's mewing.

The voice on it. Listen. Need feedin', Sam. What're we
gonnie do?

SAM

My mum'll take them.

TOM

Come on, then.

SAM

Not yet.

TOM

Eh?

SAM

We're supposed to be at school, remember? She's great my
mum. Some things though. Some things she won't tolerate.
'Jeopardizing your future.' Present pleasure future grief. I've
not had a day off school. I went to the school with my
antibiotic clutched tight in my hand, a pat on the backside,
and 'Pull yourself together,' that's what followed me down
from the doorstep. I go home now I'll get the look. You know
the look. They all do it. 'You're my beloved son and you've
wounded me to the heart.' That look's a killer. 'After all my
sacrifice.' 'I didn't ask to be born.' That's what she drives you
to. 'I didn't ask to be born.' Then she tells you. Every pain of
her labour she gives you. And the stitches they sewed her up
with. She makes you feel them every one. 'Ask', you're right,
you didn't 'ask' to be born. 'Ask?' You demanded.

I can't go home till school's well over and I've had the time
to leg it back.

Sam's putting stuff on the fire.

TOM

My mum won't have another animal in the house. Cats give
her the willies, she says. Bloody fleas, she says. I'm havin' this
one. I'm havin' it . . . Jesus, Sam.

SAM

What?

TOM

She's licking me.

SAM

Giving you a wash.

TOM

Rough tongue she's got. Think she likes me?

SAM

She'd have to be fond to lick you. I wouldn't lick you. Thinks
you need a clean. Bloody right she is too. You niff Tom
O'Halloran, d'you know that?

                              TOM
    Fanny.

                              SAM
    Eh?

                              TOM
    Her name. Fanny.

                              SAM
    Fanny?

                              TOM
    What's wrong?

                              SAM
    Callin' a cat Fanny. Shoutin' for her down the street.

                              TOM
    What's wrong with that?

                              SAM
    You dumb or what are you? Fanny?

                              TOM
    I like it.

                              SAM
    Fanny!

Tom slips the kitten down inside his shirt.

                              TOM
    Sleep, wee girl. Sleep.

He's rocking to and fro.

                              SAM
    Be singing it a bloody lullaby next. Folk should have a kitten
    delivered every three months with the milk.

He's looking at his own kitten. Slips it down inside his shirt. Laughs.

    Jesus. Bloody tickles. 'Deliver them with the milk. Make the
    world a better place.'

TOM

Dying on the beach. Jesus, Sam. Fucking mystery. Fucking
life.

Tom's eye is on the far horizon. He's very cold.

You get born. Pushed out of the house soon as look at you.
Playschool. Nursery. Learn this. Learn that. What the fuck
for, eh? They're working. You're working. I don't see them
happy. Never seen them happy. Seen them laughing, seen
that. Seen my mum rolling on the floor laughing. Frightened
me to bloody death. College. University. Work. Work. What
do they have kids for? Never fucking see them. Under my
feet. What am I supposed to do with you? I've my work. I'm
in despair. Let me bloody live.

The kitten wriggles down inside Tom's shirt. Sam laughs.

SAM

I'm gonnie be a vet. Work in a park in Africa.

TOM

Fucking park. Fucking park. That's not real. I'm gonnie pack
the shelves in fucking Safeway.

SAM

You are not.

TOM

That's what Crockett told me. Told my mum. 'I'm
disappointed in you.' That's what she said. Hired a fucking
Maths tutor. Gave him a fucking door key. Key to my house.
I get in. Mother's not there. House is cold. There's a Maths
tutor waiting for me. School nine to four. Tutor five to six.
Homework seven to nine. Bed. Nine to four. Five to six.
Seven to nine. Bed. Get up. Fucking clarinet. What do they
want? What do they fucking want? Fucking torture and you
have to thank her for it. And if you don't, she fucking cries. I
don't know. I don't know. I don't know.

Tom looks out across the ice to the mist. He cradles the kitten.

SAM
You're not gonnie pack the shelves in Safeway.

TOM
No harm in that. Eh, sweetheart? No harm at all.

Sam wanders down the beach. Picks up a stone and flings it out on the ice. Searches out flat stones. Gathers as many as he can find.

Sunlight shafts up from the ice.

DISSOLVE:

INT. THE KITCHEN/THE HALL. FRANCES'S HOUSE. DAY

The sun gleams in through the kitchen window.

Nita's filling a bowl at the sink.

Alex comes in from the breakfast room.

ALEX
What're you doing?

NITA
She's got taste, your mother. Thinking to buy this.

She lifts a porcelain bowl out of the sink. Carries it on her hip. Takes Alex by the hand. Leads him back to the fire.

ALEX
What?

NITA
Sit down.

ALEX
Nita?

NITA
Do as you're told.

He sits.

She kneels by him.

I fancied you.

122

She touches his bare foot.

ALEX

Hey.

NITA

What?

ALEX

Tickles.

NITA

I've been at that bus-stop every day. Weeks I've been there for.

She wrings the cloth out in the water. Holds the hot cloth on his foot.

Nice?

ALEX

Uh huh.

NITA

You really didn't see me? Never seen me?

He looks at her bent head. The firelight gleams on her hair.

ALEX

I wish I had.

NITA

I saw you. The moment we moved here. The furniture van was still at our door and I saw you.

She pulls the cloth between his toes.

Always wash between your toes . . . Touch me.

She turns to him. Waits. The photographs are very clear.

Touch me.

But he doesn't.

Will I wash the other foot?

ALEX

I'd like that.

123

                          NITA
    Water's not too hot?

                          ALEX
    It's fine.

                          NITA
    I'll get a towel. I'm sorry, I forgot the towel.

Alex touches her cheek.

    CUT TO:

EXT. SAM'S FIRE. DAY

Elspeth standing over Tom. Sam's far away.

                          ELSPETH
    Budge up a bit.

Tom leaps to his feet.

                          TOM
    I beg your pardon.

    CUT TO:

INT. THE HALL. DAY

Alex kisses Nita.

    CUT TO:

EXT. SAM'S FIRE. DAY

Elspeth stretching out her hand to the flames.

                          ELSPETH
    Nice fire.

                          TOM
    Yes.

                          ELSPETH
    Can I share it with you?

                              TOM
    Please.

                            ELSPETH
    I could do with a warm.

                              TOM
    I'd be delighted.

                            ELSPETH
    Is that right?

She sits.

    Good way to get piles this.

                              TOM
    I'm sorry?

                            ELSPETH
    Sitting on cold stone. Don't let me keep you from the warm.

She pats the stone beside her.

                              TOM
    Thank you.

    CUT TO:

INT. THE HALL. DAY

*Nita sits on the floor by the fire. She allows the velvet to slip off one
shoulder. Her skin's very white. There's a marble sheen to it that picks
up the firelight.*

Alex touches her shoulder.

    CUT TO:

EXT. THE LIGHTHOUSE ROCK. DAY

*Frances alone at the sea's edge. She pushes at the wedding ring on her
finger.*

    CUT TO:

INT. THE HALL. DAY

Nita allows the velvet to fall down to her waist. She sits in the firelight and lets Alex look at her.

 CUT TO:

EXT. THE LIGHTHOUSE ROCK. DAY

Frances kicking at stones. Tears streaming down her cheeks. Turning round and round. Till the world turns round her.

 CUT TO:

INT. THE HALL. DAY

Nita takes off Alex's sweatshirt.

 CUT TO:

EXT. SAM'S FIRE. DAY

Tom's staring out across the ice to the horizon.

ELSPETH

What do you see?

TOM

I don't know.

She digs in her pocket.

ELSPETH

I've treacle toffees. Would you like one?

She holds out a hand with three treacle toffees in it.

Tom takes one.

There's a pool of water round the fire.

TOM

You're very kind.

ELSPETH

One for your friend.

Tom takes the other toffee. Elspeth looks at his bent head.

Boys. I should have had a son.

CUT TO:

EXT. THE LIGHTHOUSE ROCK. DAY

Frances, eyes closed, just sitting on the rock. The world's around her.

CUT TO:

INT. THE HALL. DAY

Nita's hand touches the skin on Alex's chest. Such a light touch.

CUT TO:

EXT. SAM'S FIRE. DAY

Elspeth puts out her hand and touches Tom's cheek.

ELSPETH

Girl's are hard. Hard to rear. Hard of heart. A boy now, you
can do something with a boy. I bet . . . Is that a good toffee?

Tom's teeth are sticking together.

> TOM
>
> Very nice, thank you.

> CUT TO:

INT. THE HALL. DAY

Nita kisses Alex at the side of his mouth and then again just at the base of his neck.

> CUT TO:

EXT. THE LIGHTHOUSE ROCK. DAY

Frances turning the camera over and over in her hands.

> CUT TO:

EXT. SAM'S FIRE. DAY

Tom's watching Elspeth.

> ELSPETH
>
> I bet you've got a lot of girlfriends.

Tom manages to unstick his teeth.

> TOM
>
> Some.

> ELSPETH
>
> Have they names?

Tom decides to trust her.

> TOM
>
> Tanya.

> ELSPETH
>
> She's your girlfriend?

> TOM
>
> No chance. She'll never ask me out.

ELSPETH

Why don't you ask her?

TOM

Doesn't go like that.

ELSPETH

Try.

TOM

She's fourteen. I'm . . . Things they expect of you at fourteen. I can't . . . I'd run if she asked me out. Scared shitless I'd be.

(shrugs)

I beg your pardon.

CUT TO:

EXT. THE SHORE. DAY

Sam's throwing stones. Skiffing them across the ice. Muttering. Counting the skiffs. Throws.

SAM

One two.

CUT TO:

Frances walking round the shore. She sees Sam. Watches him collect stones.

CUT TO:

INT. THE HALL. DAY

Nita lies down on the velvet. Alex lies beside her. They begin to make love. They're gentle with each other.

CUT TO:

EXT. THE SHORE. DAY

Frances takes the lens cap off the camera. The camera comes up. A long shot of Sam throwing.

SAM

One two three.

The shutter clicks.

CUT TO:

INT. THE HALL. DAY

The photographs loom very large looking down on Alex and Nita.

Alex is looking at them. Very, very gently he holds Nita away from him.

CUT TO:

EXT. THE BEACH. DAY

Frances focuses the camera on Elspeth and Tom.

FRANCES

Do you mind if I . . .?

They turn to her.

130

Don't look. Go on talking. The way you were.

Two frozen faces look at her.

You had your hand up . . .

CUT TO:

INT. THE HALL. DAY

Alex and Nita are separate in the firelight.

                    NITA
What is it?

                    ALEX
Listen.

CUT TO:

EXT. SAM'S FIRE. DAY

                    TOM
You take snaps for a living?

                    FRANCES
Pictures.

                    TOM
You like it?

                    ELSPETH
The boy's asking you a question.

                    FRANCES
On a good day.

                    TOM
Why?

                    FRANCES
Why?

                    ELSPETH
Why?

FRANCES

I'm not telling you. I don't trust you.

ELSPETH

Would you say that to your mother? Would you?

CUT TO:

INT. THE HALL. DAY

The firelight casts shadows in the hall.

ALEX

They creak these houses. They're haunted.

NITA

They are not.

Alex pulls the velvet wrap up round Nita's shoulders.

ALEX

My dad haunts this one.

CUT TO:

EXT. SAM'S FIRE. DAY

The wind blows. Seagulls chase each other.

TOM

What do you see?

ELSPETH

What can she see, for God's sake? That's a shield she's
holding up in front of her.

FRANCES

I see you very clearly.

ELSPETH

Weddings, Frances, that's where you're headed.

FRANCES

This sees what I tell it. Often and often, it'll sniff out more.
It'll see the person if they'll let it. If I'm lucky it'll sense their
secrets too, and lay them out, every single one.

Tom digs the kitten out from inside his shirt.

TOM

Didn't see her, did it?

Elspeth laughs.

ELSPETH

Chaos, my lass. You have to open out your arms and let
chaos in. Don't you smile like that. You know all about chaos
and I know you do. I've seen your bedroom.

Frances hoots with laughter. Tom joins in.

Why's that funny? Go on, laugh, I don't care.

CUT TO:

INT. THE HALL. DAY

*Alex adjusts the photographs above the fireplace. Moving one a
fraction. Wiping dust off another.*

ALEX

I see more of my dad now than I ever did when he was alive.

Nita watches him.

Laugh. Go on. That's a joke. Right? 'I see more of my dad now.'

NITA

Come back to the fire.

ALEX

He's callin' for her. 'Frances. Frances.' He's waitin' for her. A love like theirs. Her nursing him. Doing it all for him. Used to stand by that mirror there. And her with him. Just look at himself. Her holding him. Too much skin on his body. Bloody starving to death. Arm at his back there. Hand on his arm. The two of them . . . Holding him and holding him. Till his body hurt him, so she couldn't hold him any more . . . Leaving me to look after her.

Nita gathers the velvet tight round her.

She was sleek, my mum, when he was alive. He wants her now.

CUT TO:

EXT. SAM'S FIRE. DAY

Frances stroking the kitten.

TOM

See the grey she's got under her eyes? Does her eyes the same as you.

FRANCES

So she does.

TOM

I like your eyes.

FRANCES

Thank you.

134

                              TOM
I like your hair.

                            FRANCES
You're very kind.

                              TOM
Can I have a touch?

                           ELSPETH
Will I leave you two alone?

                              TOM
Can I touch your hair?

                            FRANCES
Feel free.

Tom touches the hair at the back of her head.

                              TOM
Bristly.

                            FRANCES
Is it?

                              TOM
Tickles.

                            FRANCES
Does it?

                              TOM
Nice that. Really nice.

The gentleness of the boy's touch surprises Frances; and hurts her.

CUT TO:

INT. THE HALL/STAIRS/STUDIO. DAY

Nita's watching Alex at the photographs.

                             NITA
Take the photographs down.

ALEX

They're not mine.

NITA

It's time they came down.

She begins to take down the photographs from the mantelpiece. She does it lightly and quickly.

ALEX

They're my mother's.

But he watches her.

She runs up the stairs gathering the photographs into a bundle.

He runs up the stairs after her.

CUT TO:

EXT. SAM'S FIRE. DAY

There's a tear on Frances's cheek. She moves away from Tom's hand.

FRANCES

Are you done?

TOM

Thanks.

FRANCES

Ready?

TOM

Don't you flash that camera though. Don't you hurt her eyes.

Frances takes pictures of Tom and the kitten.

FRANCES

Beautiful eyes.

TOM

Left on the beach she was.

ELSPETH

Little thing.

136

TOM
Left her to die.

ELSPETH
Bloody *Sun* readers.

FRANCES
You don't know that.

ELSPETH
Frances, I know it. I know it like I saw them do it.

TOM
Makes you sad this weather. Makes me sad anyway.

The camera whirrs on.

ELSPETH
Sun readers. They're the ones. And you'd know it too, but
you're so damn liberal you don't know what you know.
You've forgotten how to be honest. That's what's wrong with
your photographs. *Sun* readers, I'm telling you.

The camera's at rest. She puts on the lens cap.

TOM
That it? That us done?

FRANCES
Thank you.

CUT TO:

INT. THE STAIRS. DAY

Alex takes the photographs away from Nita. He puts one back.

NITA
Don't.

*She tries to turn him towards her. A picture falls, the glass shatters. Alex
bends to pick it up. Nita slightly loses her balance.*

ALEX
Mind the glass.

137

Nita cuts her foot.

NITA

Shit.

Blood drips on to the polished wooden stair. Nita sits down.

Alex runs down the stairs to the fireside and picks up the bowl of water.

CUT TO:

EXT. SAM'S FIRE. DAY

Tom's kitten's mewing.

ELSPETH

She's hungry.

She fishes in her pocket for some money.

The cigarettes fall out. And some toffees. She doesn't notice. Tom does. He shuffles to hide the cigarettes from Elspeth.

ELSPETH

Here. You take this.

TOM

I couldn't possibly . . .

ELSPETH

Buy that baby some milk.

TOM

Thank you.

Tom tucks the kitten away. Takes the money. Palms the cigarettes.

Dropped your toffees.

Elspeth pockets the sweets.

Tom pockets the cigarettes.

CUT TO:

EXT. THE SHORE. DAY

A stone skiffs across the ice.

                    (*voice-over*)
Six seven eight nine.

Sam yells back to Tom.

   Niner! Niner!

   CUT TO:

EXT. SAM'S FIRE. DAY

                    ELSPETH
Off you go to your friend. You have fun with your friend. Tell
him . . .

Tom climbs away.

*Elspeth pokes at the fire with a stick, makes it flame. Holds a hand out
to it. Frances photographs her.*

   See through my hands. The blood running through my
   hands. That's time belting away from me. Time to cut my
   hair and have a boy touch it. A man touching me. Too many
   years. Too, too many.

                    FRANCES
Come on home. Mother. Come on.

Elspeth sits there.

   CUT TO:

EXT. THE SHORE. DAY

Tom's climbing down the rocks to Sam.

Sam throws again.

Tom's getting closer.

                    SAM
   Two three. Fuck.

And again.

Tom watches the stone rise on the ice. It disappears into the mist.

                    139

Two three four five six. Sevener. Sevener.

TOM

Sixer.

SAM

See that, did you? Bloody perfection. This bloke in America. Twenty, he can get. On water, mind. Fucking twenty. Spends all day at it. Just skiffing. That's his whole life. The perfect stone. The perfect throw.

He mimes a skiff.

TOM

My mum was school champion at the shot-put.

Tom picks up a heavy stone and puts it. He tries, really tries, to make the shot. The stone thuds down on to the ice.

Eeeeeeasy.

Sam picks one up and puts it further than Tom's.

SAM

Yes, yes, yes.

TOM

You had to do that.

SAM

Eh?

TOM

You had to fucking do it.

Tom picks up a stone and throws it. It lands short of Sam's. He keeps on heaving them, stone after stone.

SAM

What's up with you? What the fuck's goin' on? Tom?

None of the stones goes as far as Sam's. Tom's out of breath.

TOM

If you have to be fucking stupid, hey . . . Why do you have to fucking know it?

SAM

Fucking stones, Tom. What the fuck, eh?

Tom's looking out at the ice. He gets a cigarette between his teeth.

TOM

Light?

SAM

Where'd you get those?

TOM

I let an old lady touch me up. Want one?

SAM

Naaaa.

He lights Tom's. Tom climbs on to a rocky promontory and stares out into the mist. Sam lets the match burn to the bottom.

(*voice-over*)

Forgive us our debts.

DISSOLVE:

EXT. THE CREMATORIUM. DAY

The crematorium's grey and bleak. The muffled sound of 'The Lord's Prayer' comes from inside.

CONGREGATION
(*voice-over*)

As we forgive our debtors,
Lead us not into temptation.

There's a reflection of blowing clouds in the black bonnet of the ancient hearse. A black-clad driver stubs his cigarette out on the drive. Black cars line up behind him on the driveway stretching down to the great iron gates.

CUT TO:

INT. THE CREMATORIUM. DAY

Chloe's not praying. She's watching the minister blow his nose.

CONGREGATION
(voice-over)
But deliver us from evil.

Chloe stares at a candle flame. The candle's held by a young boy. He's walking towards the coffin on its plinth.

For thine is the kingdom.

Two profiles stare at the candle. Lily with satisfaction; Chloe in growing distress. The prayer ends.

The power and the glory. For ever. Amen.

The organ plays 'suitable music' for the committal.

LILY
A nice touch.

CHLOE
He's going to blow it out.

LILY
What's wrong with that?

CHLOE
I don't want him to.

Chloe stares at the candle, gnaws her lip.

EXT. THE SHORE. DAY

Tom looking through the cigarette smoke to the far mist.

SAM
Haar's coming in.

Sam dumps black seaweed on the fire. It smokes. The pods turn brown, blister and burst.

TOM
It's hard, that ice. We could go out on it.

SAM
What for?

TOM

See how far we could get.

SAM

Could break.

TOM

Fucking great stone thumping down on it, that didn't break
it.

(*silence*)

Did it?

SAM

No.

TOM

Well then?

SAM

Haar could cut us off.

TOM

You're feart.

SAM

I'm not.

TOM

Aye, you are.

SAM

Aye, I'm not.

TOM

I'm going.

SAM

I'm not stopping you.

TOM

I'll go on my own.

SAM

Go on.

                              TOM
    Right then.

                              SAM
    Right.

                              TOM
    You comin'?

                              SAM
    No.

                              TOM
    Fuck off, then.

                              SAM
    Fuck off yourself.

Tom steps out on to the ice.

Sam watches.

                              TOM
    We'll go won't we, Fanny? You and me.

He gets further out. He shouts back.

    Safe as fucking houses.

                              SAM
    Watch that kitten.

                              TOM
    She's got a fucking name.

                              SAM
    Fucking watch her, that's all.

                              TOM
    She's all right with me. I'll see no harm comes to you. Eh,
    sweetheart?

                              SAM
    Tom? Get lost in the haar! Tom?

Tom shouts back.

TOM

Fucking magic out here . . . No one else in all the world,
Fanny. Just you and me.

Gradually he's isolated.

And a warm fire waiting on the beach for when we go back. If
we go back. We could walk to another land from here. A
far-off land.

There are lights through the mist far, far away, glinting in and out.

CUT TO:

EXT. THE BEACH. DAY

There's a huge black bird hunched on the rock.

ELSPETH

What's that?

FRANCES

What does it look like?

ELSPETH

I'll not pass that.

145

FRANCES

It's a cormorant, that's all.

ELSPETH

Ill omen, Frances. That's a death bird.

Frances runs at the bird. It slowly rises in the air.

FRANCES

Alright?

The lighthouse mechanism switches on. There's a hum of electricity. The light beams out. It sweeps slowly across the empty sea.

CUT TO:

INT. THE HALL. DAY

Nita sits by the fire bathing her foot. Blood seeps through the cloth.

CUT TO:

EXT. THE SHORE. DAY

Sam's yelling from the shore; trying to see Tom through the mist.

SAM

Toooooooooooom!

Tom yells back.

TOM

Wanker.

The mist closes.

Turn your back on the shore, Fanny. See, look out there. Look far. There's nothing. Just nothing. And all the time in the world for it.

SAM

Wait for me.

TOM

Put your paws over your ears, Fanny. Had his chance. Had his bloody chance.

Tom tramps on.

SAM

Waaaaaaa-ii-t!

A blaze of sunlight on Tom. Then shade.

CUT TO:

EXT. SAM'S FIRE. DAY

Sam's wrapping the kitten in his scarf.

SAM

Stay in the warm.

Tucks it into the box.

Wait for me. You hear me? No going off with any other fucker that takes your fancy.

CUT TO:

INT. THE HALL. DAY

Alex puts more wood on the fire. The flames darken.

NITA

Make it colder.

ALEX

Flare up in a minute.

He picks up the bowl. The water's red.

I'll get fresh water.

She's left on her own at the fire. The mantelpiece is still empty.

CUT TO:

EXT. THE ICE. DAY

Sam walking far out on the ice. He looks at the scudding clouds and the gathering dark. His foot knocks a piece of loose ice. He picks it up.

SAM
　　Tom! Tom! Fucking come here!

The ice creaks.

　　Toooooooom! I'm cold to my bones!

Chucks the broken piece. It slithers a long long way.

　　Come here, wanker!

CUT TO:

EXT./INT. THE CLIFF ROAD/THE BUS. DAY

The mist is gathering in the folds of the hills. The bus has all its lights on.

Lily has a window seat. Chloe gets up from beside her and moves to the window seat in front. Lily taps her on the shoulder. Chloe won't turn round.

LILY
　　Chloe?

Chloe won't speak.

CUT TO:

EXT. THE TOWN BEACH. DAY

It's darker on the beach.

ELSPETH
　　Where's my damn cigarettes? Where are they? Have you got them?

FRANCES
　　What would I want with them?

ELSPETH
　　'What would I want with them?'

FRANCES
　　Mother!

ELSPETH

'Mother!'

(*pause*)

Och well.

FRANCES

I haven't got your cigarettes.

ELSPETH

Where are they then?

FRANCES

I don't know.

(*pause*)

Come on, Mother. I'm chilly. Take me in.

ELSPETH

Where are those boys?

FRANCES

Off on their adventures.

ELSPETH

He liked your hair. Can I feel it?

Frances bends. Her mother rubs her hand over the prickly hair at the nape of her neck.

Elspeth laughs.

Tickles right enough. Have you had a good day, cherub? I have. A rare day.

Leans against her daughter's shoulder.

They were nice boys, good boys. Think he took my cigarettes?

FRANCES

Come on in.

ELSPETH

I don't care if he did. Have you any in the house?

FRANCES

I don't smoke.

ELSPETH

I didn't ask you if you smoked. I asked you if you had any
cigarettes.

FRANCES

Yes.

ELSPETH

Have you?

FRANCES

Yes, yes. I've got some, I've got cigarettes.

ELSPETH

I'm not deaf, Frances.

FRANCES

Come and I'll give you a cigarette and I'll smoke one with
you if it'll make you happy.

ELSPETH

Are you going to Australia, Frances? Are you going to live
there?

FRANCES

It's a beautiful land.

ELSPETH

You'd miss me in Australia.

FRANCES

Like a hole in the head.

ELSPETH

Don't go to Australia.

The ice moves. Splits.

FRANCES

Mist coming in.

EXT. THE WALLED WALKWAY. DAY

*Frances walks between the grey walls up the slope of the walk. Elspeth
stops at the bottom. Leans against one wall for a moment.*

150

Frances holds out her arm to her mother.

ELSPETH

I don't need your arm. I'll manage fine without it.

FRANCES

Take my bloody arm, Mother.

There's a darkness in Elspeth and Frances sees it.

ELSPETH

My name's Elspeth.

(*pause*)

FRANCES

Take my arm Elspeth, please.

Elspeth takes it.

ELSPETH

Buy me a cup of tea. Warm me up.

Her hand is vague in the air. Frances holds it.

Maybe I'll make a table that I can leave behind me. A good
strong table with legs that I'd turned on a lathe.

Frances watches her.

Work that you can see. And when you leave it, there it is.
Don't you go away to some hot land. That's no answer,
Frances. When I'm in my box. Then you can go.

FRANCES

You're all right.

*Elspeth starts to contradict Frances. And then she doesn't. The moment
passes. Both women let it go. They walk up from the beach towards
Menzies.*

The light from the lighthouse makes its slow journey across the ice.

CUT TO:

INT. LANDING/BATHROOM DAY

Nita comes into the bathroom folding a towel. She's wearing her jeans and jumper. She puts the towel on the towel rail very gently. Picks up another from the floor.

CUT TO:

INT. THE STAIRS. DAY

Alex listens to the noises from the bathroom. Then clears the glass from the stairs with a dustpan and brush.

CUT TO:

EXT. THE ICE. DAY

The light's still circling.

Tom's kitten's caught in it. Sam crouches down, scooping Fanny into his arms.

SAM
Jesus, Fanny, where is he? He's no gone through. Has he gone through? And I cannae see. I cannae see a bloody thing.

He holds the kitten away from him.

Jesus. Help me.

The light swirls. The ice splinters.

CUT TO:

EXT. THE TERMINUS/THE PROM. DAY

A bus pulls up at the terminus. Chloe's feeling her way down its lighted aisle. Hands gripping on to each silver hand-hold.

The bus door opens. Chloe starts to run. Down the stairs and off the bus. Along the prom.

LILY
Chloe!

Chloe's caught in the lighthouse light. She stumbles.

CHLOE

Oh my God. Lily! Lily!

Chloe, eyes closed, grips on to the prom rail.

LILY

Are you all right?

CHLOE

Is that you?

LILY

For goodness sake, who do you think it is? Open your eyes, Chloe. For God's sake, what's wrong with you?

CHLOE

I fell.

LILY

You did no such thing.

CHLOE

I fell. I fell.

LILY

You hold on any tighter to that rail, the bones'll come through your skin. Where's your damn gloves, for God's sake, Chloe? Let go the rail. You're making a spectacle of yourself.

CHLOE

Who's to see?

LILY

Houses have windows, Chloe. You're in public.

CHLOE

Am I the one that's shouting, am I? Shouting and waving my arms about? That they should be looking at me. Am I?

LILY

Don't you speak to me like that.

The prom's deserted. The wind's blowing. Dark clouds are gathering behind the hill.

CHLOE

I'm standing here. That's all I'm doing. What harm is there in
that? You tell me.

LILY

I don't know what's wrong with you.

CHLOE

I fell.

LILY

It's treacherous. You slipped, that's all.

CHLOE

I let go of this. Take a finger off this. I let go. I'll fall again.

LILY

You will not.

CHLOE

That ground's waiting for me.

(*pause*)

LILY

Take my arm.

CHLOE

Bring us both down.

LILY

Do you think I can't hold you?

CHLOE

I never slipped.

LILY

We've a funeral to go to on Thursday.

CHLOE

I lost the world. As God's my witness. The world went away
from me. I didn't slip. The world fell away.

LILY

It's been a long day.

CHLOE
Lily?

LILY
I'm here.

CHLOE
You took your time getting to me, Lily. I didn't know where I was. I don't know where I am yet.

LILY
I've two pair of Arbroath smokies. All packeted up nice with their bit butter. I was saving them. We'll pop them in the pan, Chloe. A bit toast. Take my arm now. I'll not let you fall.

CHLOE
Kippers?

LILY
Arbroath smokies.

CHLOE
I don't like kippers.

LILY
Arbroath smokies, Chloe. For God's sake, are you deaf?

CHLOE
He said we were all dragonflies. That minister. When we were alive we were larva in the mud.

LILY
Larvae.

CHLOE
When we died we spread our iridescent wings in the sunshine of God's love and frolicked. That's what he said.

LILY
You take my arm.

CHLOE
What the hell did he mean?

It was a metaphor.

CHLOE

A metaphor?

LILY

Nothing wrong with a dragonfly.

CHLOE

Is that all we are, Lily? Maggots in the slime?

LILY

Didn't know what he was talking about. Did he? Did he?
Take my arm, Chloe. You'll not fall. Look at the light all
fading.

She holds out her arm.

I'm telling you, you won't fall.

Chloe puts her hand on Lily's arm.

That man had holes in his cassock, Chloe. He was overweight
and his chest was none too good. Maybe he likes dragonflies,
poor old soul. In the middle of winter. Dragonflies in the sun.

CHLOE

I don't want to be a bloody dragonfly when I die, Lily. They
only live for a day.

Lily walks Chloe along the prom.

The piano steals out on the mist.

That's all they have in the sunlight. I don't want my Heaven
to be a single day of bliss and then oblivion. I want more.

LILY

Bliss? Maybe he was a fisherman, eh? Poor old soul . . .
That's my good girl. Step by step . . . We've letters to write,
you and me . . . After all we saw her a week ago . . .
Thursday's funeral . . . We were practically in at the death
. . . You'll not fall while I'm here . . . After all what harm do
they do? Eh? Dragonflies? No harm. No harm at all.

Chloe and Lily pass Menzies just as Frances and Elspeth are coming out.

    CUT TO:

EXT. BACK DOOR/YARD. DAY

Alex watches Nita cross the backyard from the door. He nearly lets her go in silence. Then he calls after her.

                 ALEX

Will I see you again?

                 NITA

I'll be at the bus-stop.

                 ALEX

I mean see you.

                 NITA

Maybe.

She goes out the gate.

INT. KITCHEN/HALL. DAY

Alex rushes through the kitchen. The back door bangs behind him. He's heading for the stairs. In the hall by the fireplace the mantelpiece is clear of photographs. The bundle lies there, waiting to be replaced. Alex is about to do it. But he doesn't. He leaves the photographs where they are.

Runs up the stairs to the landing window.

    CUT TO:

EXT. ALEX'S POV/THE HILL. DAY

Alex watches Nita go out of the front gate and up the hill. Sees her turn and look for him. There's something between them. Maybe a nod. Maybe a smile. Then she goes on up the hill.

    CUT TO:

EXT. THE MAIN ROAD. DAY

> ELSPETH
> These photographs. These that you took today. These are good photographs.

> FRANCES
> Thank you.

Elspeth hooks her arm into her daughter's.

> I'm going to sort out the studio.

> ELSPETH
> Are you?

> FRANCES
> Maybe paint the front of the house.

> ELSPETH
> In this weather?

> FRANCES
> In the spring.

> ELSPETH
> That's good. That's very good.

Frances smiles.

The piano drifts down.

> FRANCES
> Listen.

Their heads turn.

> It's a boy playing that.

CUT TO:

EXT. THE ICE. DAY

The piano is louder.

Sam's kneeling on the ice. The light swirls over him.

SAM
Tooooooom!

CUT TO:

EXT. FRANCES'S GATE. DAY

FRANCES

What's that?

ELSPETH

Boys. Tttt. Tttt. Tttt. Tttt.

FRANCES

Are they all right?

ELSPETH

What could happen to them?

FRANCES

Shhhhh.

She stops at the railed passage.

The lighthouse beam swirls.

CUT TO:

EXT. THE LANDSCAPE. DAY

*The beam of light swirls over the whole landscape, picking out houses
and woods and streets, the rocks, the ice. Finding Sam. Lingering.
Moving on.*

The piano plays.

CUT TO:

EXT. CLIFF. DAY

*Nita goes along the cliff towards home. The shadows are deep. Faint
and far off there's a cry. A seagull maybe. Maybe a boy. She turns her
head towards the sound.*

CUT TO:

EXT. FRANCES'S BACK GATE. DAY

Frances holds the gate open for Elspeth. Frances turns and listens for a moment. The light sweeps.

ELSPETH

What?

(*pause*)

FRANCES

I don't know.

She goes down the passage to the old harbour. Elspeth follows. The wharf reaches out to the gathering darkness. Its warning light flickering at the end. Frances starts to walk towards it. The light flickers round and round.

There's a cry. Far, far away. A seagull? A boy?

Frances gives her camera to her mother. She climbs up on to the broad wharf wall, starts to run.

The piano plays.

The light fades.